"If It Makes You Feel Better," Gabe Said, "I'll Simply Explain That You And I Are An Item Again."

Alarm flared to life in Catherine's eyes. "Excuse me?"

"After all, it won't be a complete fabrication. In fact, it won't be a fabrication at all."

She tensed. "What are you talking about?"

"You never asked my price for helping you."

She inhaled sharply before lifting her chin. "How foolish of me. I'd forgotten what a pirate you are, Gabe."

"That's me," he agreed lazily. "A pirate to the bone."

"So what's your price? What do you want?"

He gave it to her hard and straight. "You. I want you, Catherine. Back in my life. Back in my apartment. And back in my bed."

Dear Reader,

I had a lot of fun writing this book. It is a lighter story than some of mine, full of emotion and humor…and of course, conflict. It's also a MAN OF THE MONTH—my first. I can't begin to express how honored I am to be included in this fantastic collection from the Silhouette Desire line.

The setting for this book is Seattle, Washington, my old stomping grounds. My son was born here and my experiences while living in this marvelous city gave birth to more than one book. A couple of years ago I was fortunate enough to visit my Totton cousins, who live in Seattle, and my mother and I had a marvelous day with them on Lake Washington. We had such a lovely day it actually provided inspiration for one of the scenes in this book.

I hope you enjoy the story, one with a tad more humor, tons of warmth, a strong, powerful hero and a heroine with a secret….

Enjoy!

Day Leclaire

DAY LECLAIRE

MR. STRICTLY BUSINESS

Published by Silhouette Books
America's Publisher of Contemporary Romance

SILHOUETTE BOOKS

ISBN-13: 978-0-373-76921-6
ISBN-10:   0-373-76921-0

Recycling programs
for this product may
not exist in your area.

MR. STRICTLY BUSINESS

Visit Silhouette Books at www.eHarlequin.com

Printed in U.S.A.

Books by Day Leclaire

Silhouette Desire

DAY LECLAIRE

USA TODAY bestselling author Day Leclaire lives and works on a remote barrier island off the North Carolina coast—a perfect setting for writing passionate books that offer a unique combination of humor, emotion and unforgettable characters. Described by Harlequin as "one of our most popular writers ever!" Day's tremendous worldwide popularity has made her a member of Harlequin's prestigious Five Star Club, with sales totaling well over five million books. She is a three-time winner of both the Colorado Award of Excellence and the Golden Quill Award. She's won a *Romantic Times BOOKreviews* Career Achievement Award and a Love and Laughter award, the Holt Medallion, a Booksellers' Best Award, and has received an impressive ten nominations for the prestigious Romance Writers of America RITA® Award.

Day's romances touch the heart and make you care about her characters as much as she does. In Day's own words, "I adore writing romances, and can't think of a better way to spend each day." For more information, visit Day on her Web site at www.dayleclaire.com.

To Jon, Louise and Samantha Totton,
with my love and gratitude, particularly for
one amazing summer day on Lake Washington.

One

"I need your help."

Gabe Piretti struggled to conceal the intense wave of satisfaction those four simple words gave him, spoken by the only woman he'd ever loved. After twenty-three months he thought he'd be able to see Catherine Haile without experiencing any lingering emotions. Foolish of him to think such a thing was even remotely possible. After all, they'd worked together. Lived together. Tangled hearts and minds and bodies into what he'd once believed an inseparable knot. The passion that erupted between them had been an inferno that even eighteen months together had done nothing to lessen. If anything, it had grown stronger with each day they'd shared.

And then she'd left. He knew the excuses she'd

offered, what she'd said or—even more damning—
hadn't said. For the first time in his life, Gabe "the
Pirate" Piretti had been unable to solve the problem. Not
by hook or crook. Not by demand, nor wit, nor full
frontal attack, nor carefully crafted stealth. When Catherine had left him, he'd lost his anchor. And as much as
he hated to admit it, he'd been adrift ever since.

If she hadn't chosen to come to him today, he'd have
seen to it that their worlds collided in the very near
future. Over the endless months they'd been apart, he'd
given her the space she'd requested. And he had watched
from a distance while she set up her business and professional life on her terms. Keeping that distance had
been the hardest thing Gabe had ever done, harder even
than when he'd swooped in and taken the helm of
Piretti's away from his mother in order to snatch the
business from the teeth of bankruptcy.

Well, now Catherine was back, and he'd find a way
to keep her. She wanted his help? So be it. He'd give it
to her. But the price would be high. The question
was…would she pay it, or would she run again?

Aware that he'd kept her standing, Gabe waved her
toward the sitting area that occupied a large corner of
his office. Liquid sunlight, still damp from a recent
shower, spilled in through tinted glass windows that
overlooked a broad sweep of Seattle, as well as Puget
Sound. The brilliant rays caught in Catherine's up-
swept hair, picking out the streaks of gold buried in the
honey warmth.

"Coffee?" he offered.

After taking a seat, Catherine set her briefcase at her feet and shook her head. "I'm fine, thanks."

He took the chair across from her and tilted his head to one side as he studied her. She wore a chocolate-brown silk suit that shimmered richly over subtle curves, revealing that she'd recently lost weight, weight she could ill-afford to lose. The fitted jacket nipped in at a miniscule waist and ended just shy of a feminine pair of hips. She'd chosen sandals that were little more than a knot of sexy straps with the prerequisite three-inch heels, which she invariably wore to give the illusion of height. The heels also performed double duty by showcasing a stunning pair of legs. Clearly, she'd dressed to impress...or distract.

"It's been a while," he commented. "You've changed."

"Stop it."

He lifted an eyebrow and offered a bland smile. "Stop what?"

"You're mentally undressing me."

It was true, though not the way she thought. He couldn't help but wonder what had caused the recent weight loss, but was careful to hide his concern beneath gentle banter. "Only because I figured you'd object if I undressed you any other way."

A reluctant smile came and went. "What happened to your motto of strictly business?"

"When it comes to work, I am all business." He paused deliberately. "But you don't work for me, do you?"

"And haven't for three and a half years."

His humor faded. "Do you regret your choices, Catherine?"

He caught a flicker of distress before she rearranged her expression into a mask of casual indifference. "Some of them. But that's not what you're asking, is it? You want to know if I had the opportunity to do it over again, would I choose differently?" She gave it serious consideration. "I doubt it. Some things you simply have to experience in order to learn how to live your life…or how not to."

"Some things? Or some people?"

She met his gaze, dead-on. "Both, of course. But I'm not here to discuss our past."

"Straight to business, then."

She continued to study him. He remembered how disconcerting he'd found those amber-gold eyes when they'd first met. Nothing had changed. They were still as intense as they were unusual, seeing far more than he felt comfortable revealing. "Isn't business first how you prefer it?" she asked. "I seem to recall that's practically a cardinal rule at Piretti's. Whenever you buy and sell companies, put them together or dismantle them, it's never personal. It's just business."

"Normally, that would be true. But with you…" He shrugged, conceding the unfathomable. "You were always the exception."

"Funny. I'd have said just the opposite."

Her mouth compressed, a habitual gesture when the spontaneous part of her nature ran up against the bone-deep kindness that kept her more wayward thoughts in check. In the past, he'd taken great delight in kissing those wide, full lips apart and teasing the truth from her.

Somehow he didn't think she'd respond well to that particular tack. Not now. Not yet.

"Sorry," she murmured. "Water under the bridge."

"Quite a bit of water. But not quite enough to break the dam. I'll have to see what I can do about that."

A hint of confusion drifted across her expression, but he moved on before she could question what he meant. In time, he'd find out why she'd left. In time, he'd break through that calm, polite facade and force the fury and passion to the surface. He'd poke and prod until the dam finally broke and the truth spilled out.

"How have you been?" he asked, hoping the mundane question would help her relax.

A hint of strain blossomed across her elegant features. When he'd first met her—and hired her on the spot—he'd thought her delicate. And though her fine-boned appearance gave that impression, he'd quickly learned she possessed a backbone of steel. But right now she seemed more than delicate. She looked undone.

"I'm a little stressed right now," she confessed. "Which is why I'm here."

"Tell me about it," he prompted.

She hesitated, gathering her self-control and wrapping dispassion around herself like a protective cloak. "About eighteen months ago, I started my own business."

"Elegant Events."

He'd surprised her. "How did—" She waved the question aside. "Never mind. You would have made it your business to know what I did after we went our separate ways."

"You mean…after you left me."

The correction escaped without thought or intent, the words whisper-soft and carrying an underlying edge. An edge she caught. The strain she fought so hard to conceal deepened, melded with an old anger and an even older hurt. Her hands curled tight, her knuckles bleached white. This time when she compressed her mouth he suspected it was to control the betraying tremble. Time stretched taut.

"Do you really want to go there?" she asked at last. She pinned him with a single look. "Do we need to deal with the past now? Is that the only way you're willing to help me?"

"It's not the only way."

"Just the way you prefer." She didn't wait for the confirmation. "Fine. I'll make this as straightforward as I know how. You, with your unrelenting need to keep business and personal in separate compartments, gave me a choice. I could work for you or love you, but not both. I, foolishly, chose love. What I didn't realize is that you were already in love. And that love would always come first with you."

"You were the only woman in my life," he bit back.

She lifted a shoulder and smiled in a way that threatened to tear his heart right out of his chest. "Perhaps the only woman, but not the only thing. Piretti's was always your first love. And because of that, it will always be the love you put first."

"You left me because I worked late on occasion?"

he demanded in disbelief. "Because sometimes I was forced to put work ahead of you or our social life?"

She didn't bother arguing, though he could see part of her yearned to. The anger and disillusionment could be read in her expression, the bitter words trembling on the tip of her tongue. She waited until both faded away before speaking.

"Yes," she said with painful simplicity. "Yes, I left you for all those reasons."

"And a host of others?" he guessed shrewdly.

She inclined her head. "And a host of others." Before he could demand more information, she held out a hand in supplication. "Please, Gabe. It's been nearly two years. There's no point in beating this issue to death after all this time. Can't we move on?" She paused a beat, a hint of wry humor catching him by surprise. "Or am I wasting my time coming here today?"

He had no intention of moving on, but he could be patient. Maybe. If he tried really hard. "You aren't wasting your time. If it's in my power to help, I will. Why don't you start by explaining the problem to me?"

She took a deep, steadying breath. "Okay, let's see if I can't keep this short and straightforward, the way you like it. In a nutshell, Elegant Events is an event-staging business geared toward upper-echelon corporations and large-budget clientele."

"Of which there are plenty in the Seattle area."

She nodded. "Exactly. My goal was—and is—to plan and stage every aspect of the event in order to spare clients any and all worry and headaches. They tell me what they want, and I provide it. If they're willing to pay for it, I'll find a way of fulfilling their every desire, and if possible, to exceed their expectations."

"And you do it with grace and elegance and panache."

Pleasure gave her cheeks a hint of much-needed color. "You should write my PR releases. That's precisely our goal. We strive to bring something unique to every event, to set the perfect stage, whether it's to highlight the release of a new product or to create the perfect memory for a special, once-in-a-lifetime occasion."

"Like the Marconi affair tonight."

She shook her head in amused disbelief. "Is there anything you don't know? Yes, like the Marconi affair tonight. You're only ninety once, and Natalie is under tremendous pressure to make her father-in-law's birthday celebration an unforgettable occasion."

Gabe couldn't remember the last time he'd seen Catherine so happy, and that fact filled him with regret. She'd suffered at his hands. It hadn't been deliberate on his part, but that didn't alter the facts. "I don't doubt you'll pull the party off in grand style," he stated with absolute conviction.

"During my years at Piretti's, as well as during the time we were together, I learned a lot about what works, and more importantly, what doesn't. And though I didn't expect the business to take off right away, to my surprise and delight, it did." Energy and enthusiasm rippled through her voice. "We've scored some impressive clients and they seemed pleased with the various events. At least, I thought they were."

Her excitement dimmed and he frowned in concern. "Obviously, something's gone wrong. What's happened to change all that?"

The last of her vivaciousness drained away, leaving behind the tension. "Two things. First, we're losing clients. It's nothing overt. Just contracts I thought were a sure thing have suddenly gone away without any explanation. Everyone's polite and makes encouraging noises, but when it's all said and done, they choose another company."

"And the second problem?"

"Is the most serious." Worry darkened her eyes and turned her voice husky with nerves. "We're on the verge of bankruptcy, Gabe. And I don't know why. I thought we'd been careful with our profit margin, but maybe there's been more waste than I realized. I can't quite get a handle on it. It's not my area of expertise. I can tell something's off, but I can't seem to pinpoint what. I'm hoping you can figure it out and suggest changes to correct the problem before we go under."

He keyed in on one very pertinent word that he hadn't noticed until then. "We?" he repeated.

She hesitated. "I have a partner, someone who prefers to remain anonymous," she hastened to add.

He didn't like the sound of that. "Why?"

Catherine lifted a shoulder. "She just does. Since half the startup money was hers, I respect her desire for privacy."

She. Gabe refused to allow his relief to show that the partner was female rather than a male. It was petty of him, but he couldn't seem to help himself. Not when it came to Catherine. Still, it seemed odd that this partner would want to keep her identity a secret. Maybe he'd do a little digging and see if he couldn't find out what the mystery was all about. "Depending on what I find, that may need to change," he warned. "There's an excellent chance I'll want to meet her."

"I did discuss that possibility with her. She's agreed that if it means the difference between salvaging the business and having Elegant Events go bankrupt, she's willing to meet with you."

"Good decision," he said dryly.

"Agreed." A quick smile flashed. He didn't realize how much he missed it until it was there, reawakening an ache that had been tamped down, but never fully excised. "Tell me what you require in order to get started," she requested.

He forced himself to switch gears. "All bank and accounting records since you opened your doors." He ran through a mental list. "Debts, creditors, cost of goods purchased, billables, write-offs. Your prospectus, past and current contracts, a list of services offered and what you charge for them."

"In other words, you want a copy of everything." She reached for her briefcase. Pulling out a thick folder, she handed it to him. "I have most of that information with me."

He nodded. "Excellent. I'll go over what you brought and have Roxanne prepare a list of anything more I might need."

A shadow swept across Catherine's face, evaporating so swiftly that he'd have missed it if he hadn't been looking straight at her. "I'd hoped to keep my problem strictly between the two of us. Would you mind if we leave your assistant out of this? Is that possible?"

"Possible, but not probable. Roxanne is privy to most of what goes on around here."

"And what she isn't privy to, I'm certain she makes it her business to find out," Catherine commented blandly. "How else can she provide you with everything you need?"

Okay, he knew a minefield when he saw one. "I'll leave Roxanne out of the loop."

"And if she asks?"

His eyes narrowed. "Are you questioning how I run my business? Considering why you're here…"

"No, I—"

"I didn't think so." He relented. "But if it will make you feel better, should the subject come up in conversation, I'll simply explain that you and I are an item again."

Alarm flared to life in Catherine's eyes. "Excuse me?"

"After all, it won't be a complete fabrication." He smiled in anticipation. "In fact, it won't be a fabrication at all."

She tensed, like a mouse finally noticing the trap. She'd been so busy nibbling at the tasty hunk of cheese that she'd been oblivious of it. Until now. "What are you talking about?"

"You never asked my price for helping you."

She inhaled sharply before lifting her chin. "How foolish of me. I'd forgotten what a pirate you are, Gabe."

"That's me," he agreed lazily. "A pirate to the bone."

"So what's your price? What do you want?"

He gave it to her hard and straight. "You. I want you, Catherine. Back in my life. Back in my apartment. And back in my bed."

She shot to her feet. "You've lost your mind. You can't possibly think I'd agree to such a thing."

He regarded her in silence for a long moment before responding. "I guess that depends on how badly you want to save your business."

"Not that badly."

He stood and closed the distance between them. "Liar."

"Whatever there was between us is over, Gabe. Dead."

She was so small compared to him. So delicately put together. And yet she vibrated with sheer feminine outrage, with a strength and power he found irresistible. It was one of the qualities he'd always admired about her. Where most women looked for ways to make themselves as appealing to him as possible, Catherine had never played those types of games. He'd always known where he stood with her. Those gloriously unique eyes of hers could slay him with a single look, or melt him with the fire of her passion. Right now she was busy slicing and dicing him in every imaginable way.

"I know you'd like to think that what we shared is dead and buried." He allowed his amusement to show. "But you've forgotten one small detail."

"What detail?" she demanded.

"This…"

He slid his arms around her and locked her close

against him. He remembered the feel of her, the perfect way her body fit his. She had a pixie-lean figure with delicious curves her trim business suit only hinted at. But they were there, and they never failed to arouse him. Unable to resist, he cupped her face and drew her up for a kiss. She didn't fight as he expected, but neither did she respond. Not that he expected instant capitulation. That would take time.

For now, her full, generous mouth did no more than accept the teasing pressure of his. Gently, oh so gently, he teased his way past that sweet barrier, knowing just how she liked to be touched. Caressed. Taken. He'd missed the taste of her, the feel of her, the subtle scent of her. He missed the sharpness of her mind, and yes, even the sharpness of her tongue when she felt wronged.

He missed the quiet evenings when they'd sit together on his balcony sipping a glass of local merlot while day slid into night and Puget Sound came alive with the twinkling lights from the boat and ferry traffic. How they would slip from soft, sweet conversation to a soft, sweet tangle of arms and legs and lips. How their clothes would form a silken pathway from the balcony to the bedroom. And then the night would go from that softness, that sweetness, to something fiery and demanding. Something that branded their connection on every fiber of his being.

No matter how hard he tried to cut off that part of himself, that part indelibly linked to her, it would have been easier to rip out his heart and soul. He couldn't live without her. And he wouldn't. He'd been one of the living dead for long enough. He refused to spend another minute without Catherine in his life. And if it meant that he had to use blackmail to get her there, then that's what he'd do. Because once he had her back, he'd do whatever necessary to keep her.

With a soft moan, her lips parted and he slid inward. For a split second she surrendered to him, taking all he had to give. Her body flowed against his and her lips moved with familiar certainty, nibbling hungrily. Her fingers slid into his hair and gripped, anchoring them together. And her heeled foot inched upward, hooking around his calf in a practiced maneuver. He recognized the signal and responded without thought. Cupping her bottom, he lifted her so she could wrap those incredible legs around his waist. The instant he did, she began to fight free.

"No!" She wriggled from his hold and took several stumbling steps backward. "This isn't happening."

"It's too late, Catherine. It already happened."

He saw comprehension burn in her eyes. He also caught an infuriated acknowledgment that their feelings for each other weren't anywhere near as dead as she claimed, though if he didn't miss his guess, that fury was aimed more at herself than at him. She closed her eyes, effectively shutting him out.

"Damn," she whispered.

"Does that kiss prove my point, or is another demonstration necessary?"

She yanked at the hem of her suit jacket and with an exclamation of annoyance, shoved button through hole where it had come undone. Then she tugged at her skirt and smoothed her hair. What he'd ruffled, she swiftly unruffled. Then she regarded him with undisguised irritation. "You've made your point," she retorted. He could only imagine the amount of effort it took to look at him. "You do realize that I believed it was over between us, or I'd never have approached you."

"That's rather naive of you since there's not a chance in hell this will ever be over between us, sweetheart."

Her chin shot up. "There shouldn't have been anything left. I figured at most we'd have to kick over some of the ashes just to satisfy our morbid curiosity. I didn't expect to find any lingering embers."

"I don't doubt that for a minute."

"This—" She waved an all-encompassing hand to indicate him, herself, and the kiss that still heated their lips. "None of it changes my mind about our relationship. I'm not coming back home."

Home. The slip hung in the air for a timeless instant. He didn't reply. He simply smiled knowingly.

Swearing beneath her breath, she shot toward the couch and gathered up the file she'd given him and stuffed it inside her briefcase. Tossing the strap of her purse over one shoulder, she spun around to face him. He deliberately stood between her and the door. Not that that stopped her.

"I'm leaving," she warned. "And I'm going around you, through you or over your dead body. But I am going."

"And I'm going to make certain that doesn't happen. Oh, not today," he reassured her at her unmistakable flare of alarm. "But very soon I'm going to be around you, through you and—trust me—your body will be far from dead when I'm over it." He stepped to one side. "When you change your mind about needing my help with Elegant Events, you know where to find me."

She crossed the room, circling just out of reach as she headed for the door. Her hand closed over the knob, and then she hesitated. "Why, Gabe?" she asked quietly, throwing the question over her shoulder. "Why the conditions?"

"The truth?"

"If you don't mind."

The words escaped in a harsh undertone, the brutal honesty making them all the more devastating in their delivery. "Not a night passes that I don't ache for you, Cate. Not a morning dawns that I don't reach for you. I want the pain to end. The next time I reach out, I want you there."

Two

It took every ounce of self-possession for Catherine to exit Gabe's office without it looking as though she were attempting to escape the fiery pits of hell. Worse, she'd completely forgotten about Roxanne Bodine, aka Satan's handmaiden, whose sharp black eyes made note of the distress Catherine wasn't quick enough to conceal. A mocking smile slid across sharply flamboyant features.

"Not the reunion you were hoping for?" Roxanne asked in a honeyed voice that contained just a whiff of a southern drawl. "If you'd bothered to ask, I could have warned that you were wasting your time. You let that fish slip off your hook nearly two years ago, and he's none too eager to slip back on again."

"Maybe you should tell him that," Catherine retorted, then wanted to kick herself for revealing so much.

Roxanne could deliver taunts with needle-sharp precision. But she wasn't the type of woman who took them well. Nor did she appreciate the implication that Gabe might be interested in getting back together with the rival she'd worked so hard to rid herself of.

"Some women don't understand the concept of making a graceful exit." Roxanne stood and stretched a figure as full and lush as Catherine's was petite and fine-boned. She settled on the corner of her desk with all the lazy grace of a true feline. Then she proceeded to sharpen her claws on the nearest available target, in this case, Catherine. "Seems to me you'd have more pride than to come crawling back. You're just asking to get kicked to the curb again."

All her life Catherine had chosen discretion over a more overt approach. She'd been the good girl. Quiet. Polite. Turning the other cheek when required. But enough was enough. She didn't have anything to lose anymore. "I don't know how I'd survive without you looking out for my welfare, Roxanne," Catherine said with a sunny smile. "Maybe that's your problem. Maybe instead of looking out for me, you should be looking out for yourself."

"Oh, don't trouble yourself on my account. I'm like a cat," she said, stating the all-too obvious. "I've been blessed with nine lives and I have a knack for landing on my feet."

Catherine planted a hand on a trim hip. "And yet here you are still sitting behind a desk...like an alley cat meowing at the back door waiting to be let in. I'd have thought with me out of the way, you'd have found a way in by now. I guess that's one door you can't quite slink through."

Fury turned Roxanne's face a deadly shade of white while two patches of harsh red streaked across her sharp cheekbones. "You think I made your life a misery before? Try me now. This is my turf, and I'll do whatever necessary to defend it."

Catherine made a sweeping gesture. "Go right ahead. But while you're so busy staking out your territory, maybe you should consider one small detail that you seem to have overlooked."

That stopped her. "I haven't overlooked a thing," Roxanne insisted, just a shade too late.

"No? How about this. You know your boss. When he wants something, he doesn't let anything stand in his way. Gabe wants, Gabe takes." Catherine allowed that to sink in before continuing. "You've worked for him for…what? Two and a half years? Three? And yet you've never been taken. I'm willing to bet you can't even get him to sample the goods. If he hasn't been tempted in all that time, what makes you think he ever will?"

She didn't wait for a response. If there was one thing she'd learned since opening Elegant Events, it was when to pack up your knives and leave. Without another word, she swung around and headed for the elevators. The instant she stepped into the car, she checked her back. To her relief she didn't find any of those knives sticking out of it.

Yet.

* * *

"So, fill me in on every detail. How did it go?" Dina Piretti asked eagerly. "You didn't have to tell him about me, did you?"

Catherine set down her briefcase just inside the front door and shot Gabe's mother an uneasy glance. "No, he still hasn't discovered that you're my partner," she reassured her.

Dina released a sigh. "I hear a 'but' in there."

"But it didn't go well," Catherine confessed. "I'm afraid we're on our own. We'll either have to figure out where the problem is ourselves, or we'll have to hire an outside consultant to advise us. A consultant other than your son."

Dina stared in patent disbelief. "No," she stammered. "You must have misunderstood. I can't believe Gabriel refused to help you. Not you."

Catherine hesitated. She had two choices. She could lie, something she not only hated, but didn't do well. Or she could tell Gabe's mother what her precious firstborn had demanded in exchange for his help. Neither option held any appeal.

"I need a drink," she announced. Maybe while they fixed a pot of coffee, some stroke of brilliance would come to her and she'd figure out a third option. "And then we'd better get to work. The Marconi birthday party is tonight and I have a dozen phone calls I need you to make while I head over there and supervise the setup."

Dina led the way to her kitchen, though she hardly needed to considering the two women spent a good deal of their workday together in its comfortable confines.

When they'd first conceived Elegant Events it had been right here, in Dina's Queen Anne home, sitting at her generously sized bleached oak kitchen table. Since then, they'd filled the emptiness of the huge house by converting several of the rooms into an office suite, one that had so far escaped Gabe's notice. The division of labor worked to each of their strengths. Catherine manned the front lines, while Dina ran the business end of things. Right now the older woman wore her shrewdest and most businesslike expression.

"You're being evasive, Catherine. That's not like you. Tell me what went wrong. Oh, wait. I'll bet I can guess." A broad smile flashed, one identical to Gabe's. When they'd first started working together that smile had caused Catherine untold pain. Even now it stirred a twinge that wouldn't be denied. "Gabriel put those patented Piretti moves on you, didn't he?"

Catherine deliberately turned her back on her partner. "One or two," she admitted. Dumping fresh coffee beans into the grinder, she switched it on, relieved that the noise of the machine made conversation impossible.

The instant the machine shut off, Dina jumped in. "It was just the same with his father. I never could resist him." A hint of sorrow appeared in her eyes and cut faint grooves beside her mouth. Not that it detracted from her startling beauty, a beauty she'd managed to pass on to her son, if in a slightly more masculine form. "Funny how much I can still miss him after all this time."

Catherine abandoned the coffee and wrapped her arms around Dina. "From everything you and Gabe have told me, he was an incredible man. I only wish I could have met him."

"He'd have adored you." Dina pulled back and forced a smile. "You've evaded answering me long enough. What happened? Why did Gabriel refuse to help?"

"He didn't refuse," Catherine told her. "He just put a price on his help that I'm unwilling to pay."

"Ah." Understanding dawned. "He wanted to get back together with you, didn't he?"

"How did you…?" Catherine's eyes narrowed. "Did you speak to him before I went over there?"

"I haven't spoken to Gabriel about you in months. I haven't spoken to him at all in the past three days," Dina insisted. She crossed to the coffee machine and made short work of starting the brewing process before turning to face Catherine. "I am, however, a woman, and I know my son. He's still in love with you."

No, not love, Catherine almost said. Lust, maybe. But he'd never truly been in love with her. Not that she could explain any of that to Dina. "He said that he'd only help if I moved back in with him."

"Naturally, you refused."

"Naturally."

"Because you don't have feelings for him anymore, either."

Catherine didn't dare answer that one. Instead, she regarded Dina with troubled eyes. "I know you've always hoped that we'd work out our differences, but that's not going to happen. You understand that, don't you?"

It was Dina's turn to look troubled. "I've never wanted to push for answers you weren't ready to give. I gather something went horribly wrong between you. You were so ill during those early weeks after the two of you broke up that I didn't have the heart to ask. But I always thought that you and Gabriel would work it out. You were so right together. So in love." She swept that aside with a wave of her hand. "Never mind. You were absolutely right to refuse him. It was quite rude of Gabriel to put conditions on his help."

Catherine smiled in relief. "You're not upset?"

"I'm disappointed." She poured them both a cup of freshly brewed coffee, putting an end to the subject. "Why don't we forget about all that for now and get down to business? I suggest we double- and triple-check that everything's in place for tonight's affair. We can't afford any errors."

No question about that. Between their financial woes and the contracts they'd lost, there was added urgency on getting every event perfect. The next several hours flew by. Much to Catherine's relief, the intensity of the work didn't allow for thoughts of Gabe to intrude. Every ounce of concentration and effort went into putting the finishing touches on the Marconi event. More than ever she needed tonight to be a stunning success, for Natalie Marconi to rave about Elegant Events to all of her closest friends—and more importantly, her husband's business contacts.

By nine that night the party was in full swing, and Catherine worked behind the scenes, keeping everything running with smooth efficiency, while remaining as unobtrusive as possible. Having a half dozen walkie-talkies that kept all the various stations in touch with each other certainly helped with speed and communication, not to mention coordinating the progress of the party. But she always faced last-minute glitches, and tonight proved no exception.

This time around the band showed up late and the caterers underestimated the amount of champagne necessary to fill the flutes of the several hundred people who'd come to toast the Marconi patriarch. Both problems were corrected before anyone noticed, but it took some fast maneuvering, a flurry of phone calls and an exhausting combination of threats and pleas.

Catherine paused by the doorway leading outside to the staging area and, for what seemed like the fiftieth time that night, examined the checklist she'd posted there. Every aspect of the evening was listed and carefully initialed by the responsible party once it had been dealt with. She'd found the list a lifesaver on more than one occasion since it kept everyone up to date on the progress of the event, and ensured accountability. Only a few boxes remained blank. The birthday cake. A few catering chores. And, of course, the post-party cleanup.

Satisfied, she had started toward the kitchen to speak with the caterers about the cake when she felt a telltale prickle along her spine. She turned, not the least surprised to discover Gabe lounging in the doorway behind her.

For a split second, all she could do was stand and stare. That's how it had been the first time she'd seen him, too. One look stole every last ounce of sense and sensibility. He stood a full six feet two inches, with mile-wide shoulders, topping a powerful, toned body. He'd encased all that potent masculinity in formal wear, which turned his body into a lethal weapon that no woman had a chance of resisting. But it was far worse than that. Gabe Piretti also possessed the striking features of an angel coupled with the burning cobalt-blue eyes of a devil. And right now he had those predatory eyes fixed on her.

It wasn't just the raw, physical impact of the man, Catherine was forced to admit. Perhaps for some women that would be sufficient. Maybe his looks, along with the embarrassing number of digits that graced his bank account, would satisfy. But she'd always wanted something else in the man she chose as her own. She wanted a heart and a mind that worked in sync with hers. For a brief time, she'd found that with Gabe. At least, she had until he made it clear that money was his god, and what she had to offer was only icing to fill in the cracks of his multi-layered cake.

Maybe he hadn't caught her helpless reaction to his appearance, though why she even bothered to indulge in such pointless speculation, she didn't know. One glimpse of the amusement gleaming in his eyes put paid to that forlorn hope. How could she have forgotten? Gabe could read people at a single glance. It was part of what made him such a good deal-broker. No one pulled anything over on him.

Except Roxanne.

"Should I even bother to ask what you're doing here?" she asked.

A half smile eased across his mouth. "I was invited."

"Of course." She didn't doubt that for a minute. "You neglected to mention it when I saw you this morning."

He lifted a shoulder in a careless shrug. "Must have slipped my mind." His attention switched to her mouth. "I believe I was preoccupied with more important matters at the time."

"Speaking of more important matters, I have to work right now. So if you'll excuse me…" She started to press past him, but he shifted just enough to make it awkward. "Gabe, please," she whispered. "This is a really bad idea."

"I'm afraid I have to disagree with you about that." When she made another move to pass him, he pressed her against the wall, locking her in place. Tucking a loosened curl of hair behind her ear, he allowed his fingers to drift from the curve of her cheek to her mouth. And there, he lingered. "Just give me one more minute."

"Forget it, Gabe. I can't be caught necking with the guests."

"I just want to talk to you. You can spare a minute to talk, can't you?"

One minute. Sixty seconds of sheer heaven. She couldn't resist the temptation, not when those devil's eyes promised such decadent delight. "You can have thirty seconds. But no kissing the help," she warned.

His smile came slow and potent. "You look stunning tonight. That shade of bronze turns your eyes to pure gold."

It took her precious seconds to find her voice and respond with anything approaching normalcy. "I look quietly elegant," she corrected in far too husky a voice. "I work hard at looking quietly elegant so that I fit in with my surroundings without standing out."

He regarded her in amusement. "I gather standing out would be inappropriate."

"It would," she assured him.

Just another few seconds and then she'd step away from him. She'd step away and force her mind back to business. Just another moment to feel the powerful press of his body against hers. To gather up his unique scent and allow it to seep into her lungs. To lower her guard just this one time and surrender to the stir of memories, memories of what once was and what could have been, if only…

She snatched a deep breath, forcing herself to address the mundane and irreverent. With luck it would help her regain her sanity, something she'd clearly lost. "I don't want to wear something too flashy, any more than I want to wear clothing too casual for the occasion. I want the attention on the event and the participants, not on me."

"I can see your dilemma." He continued to stand close, so close that she could feel the softness of his breath against her skin. "There's only one small problem with your scenario."

"Which is?" she managed to ask.

"You could be in a burlap sack and you'd still outshine every woman here."

She shouldn't allow his flattery to affect her. And maybe she wouldn't have if she hadn't witnessed the flare of passion in his eyes and heard the ring of sincerity in his voice. She weakened, just for an instant, her body and heart softening. Yielding.

It was all the invitation he needed. He leaned into her, pressing her against the wall. And then he consumed her. If she thought the kiss they'd shared earlier had threatened to overwhelm her, it was nothing compared to this one. He knew just how to touch her to decimate every last ounce of control. He breached her defenses and slipped inside with an ease that shook her to the core.

And in that moment, he turned her world upside down.

She heard a harsh groan and couldn't tell if it emanated from his throat or hers. All she knew was that it sounded primal and desperate. She'd gone without this for too long, she was forced to concede. She'd been stripped of something she hadn't even realized she needed. He was her air. Her heartbeat. Her sustenance and her reason for being. How had she survived all this time without him?

Unable to help herself, she wrapped herself around him and gave. And then she gave more, putting all the longing and hope and despair into that one single kiss. She had no idea how long they stood there, their breath coming in urgent pants, hands groping, bodies pressing.

Perhaps she'd never have surfaced if she hadn't suddenly felt a tingling awareness that they were being watched. Shoving at his shoulders, she pushed him back, or tried to, for all the good it did her. The man was as immovable as an oak, and because of his height, he blocked her view of whomever had witnessed their embrace. All she caught was a fleeting glimpse of red.

"Playtime's over," she managed to say.

It took him a minute to release her and another one after that for her to recover her equilibrium and attempt to walk down the hallway. Thank God she'd worn sensible shoes. If she'd tried to maneuver on her usual heels, her shaky legs would have pitched her straight onto her backside. He must have picked up on the results of his handiwork because his rumble of laughter followed her down the hallway, as did he.

"Seriously, I need to work, Gabe," she said, attempting to dismiss him. She gave her walkie-talkie a cursory check to make sure she hadn't accidentally bumped the volume knob. To her relief, she saw that it was on and working just fine.

"I won't get in your way. I have a legitimate reason for following you."

"Which is?"

"I need to watch how your run your business. Just in case."

"Just in case...what?" she asked distractedly.

"Just in case you change your mind and ask for my help."

She stopped dead in her tracks and faced him. "That isn't going to happen. I can't meet your price." She shook her head. "Correction. I *won't* meet it."

He only had to lift a single eyebrow for her to consider what had happened just moments ago, and realize that her claim rang a little hollow. "Time will tell," he limited himself to saying.

She waved him aside with an impatient hand and

looked around, not sure where she was or how she'd gotten there. What the hell had she been going to do when he'd interrupted her? She was utterly clueless. With an irritated sigh, she turned on her heel and headed back the way she'd come. Giving the checklist another cursory glance, she stepped outside. She'd do a quick walk-through and inspect each of the various stations. Then she'd touch bases with the caterers— She snapped her fingers. The caterers. That's where she'd intended to go. She needed to coordinate the presentation of the cake.

She spared Gabe a brief glance. If she turned around yet again, she'd confirm how thoroughly he'd rattled her, which would never do. No point in giving him that much of an advantage. Instead, she'd keep moving forward and circle back once she'd ditched him. She crossed the beautifully manicured lawn toward Lake Washington, pausing at the demarcation between grass and imported white sand. She took a moment to gaze out across the dark water. And all the while a painful awareness surged through her.

"You've done an incredible job, Catherine," Gabe said quietly. "The gondolas are a particularly special touch. I'm sure it reminds Alessandro of his home in Italy."

Catherine smiled at the sight of the distinctive boats and the gondoliers manning them, all of whom were decked out in their traditional garb of black slacks, black-and-white-striped shirts and beribboned straw hats. Some were even singing as they rowed, maneuvering the distinctive single oar with impressive skill and dexterity as they ferried passengers around the section of the lake cordoned off for their use. Channel markers fashioned to look like floating fairy lights turned the scene into a romantic wonderland.

"It was something Natalie said that made me think of it," Catherine explained. "I was a bit concerned about lake traffic, but we were able to get permission to use this small section for a few hours tonight. I even stationed security personnel in private craft directing boaters away from the area."

"Smart, though there's a no-wake zone through here, isn't there?"

"There's supposed to be." She shrugged. "But you know how that can go."

Satisfied that the guests were thoroughly enjoying their small taste of Venice, she turned her attention to the buffet station set up on one side of the sweeping lawn. The caterers she'd chosen specialized in authentic Italian cuisine and had gone all out for the evening's festivities. Graceful tents of silk and tulle surrounded the groaning tables. With a stiff breeze blowing from off the lake, the tents served the duel function of protecting the food and keeping the fuel canisters beneath the hot dishes from blowing out. Adjacent to the tents, linen draped tables dotted the area, the silver cutlery and crystal glassware gleaming softly beneath the lighting.

Catherine gave the area one final check, and was on the verge of returning to the kitchen when she caught sight of Roxanne. The woman stood chatting with Natalie, while her gaze roamed the crowds, clearly searching for someone. Catherine could make three big, fat guesses who that someone might be and they would all center on the man standing beside her.

"I didn't realize you brought your assistant with you," she said to Gabe.

He followed her gaze and shrugged. "I didn't. I believe she's a friend of Natalie's daughter."

As though aware of the scrutiny, Roxanne homed in on Catherine...and Gabe. And then her lips curved in a killer smile, a horribly familiar one that, in the past, warned of coming trouble. Offering her hostess a quick air kiss, she excused herself and made her way toward them, undulating across the grass with her distinctive catwalk stride.

She looked fabulous, Catherine reluctantly conceded, dressed in traffic-stopping red. The bodice of her skin-tight dress bared a path of bronzed skin straight to her equator while her skirt barely covered the assets composing her southern hemispheres. She shot Catherine a challenging look, before wrapping herself around Gabe.

"Since we're not on duty..." She moistened her lips before planting a lingering kiss on his mouth. Then she pulled back and laughed up at him. "See what you've been missing? I did tell you."

He regarded his assistant with indulgent amusement. "A shame I have that rule about not mixing business with pleasure," he replied easily. "Otherwise, you'd be in serious trouble."

"Some rules are made to be broken. And in case you didn't notice, I excel at trouble." Her dark eyes sparkled. "Don't you agree?"

"That you excel at trouble?" He inclined his head. "Absolutely. Unfortunately, my rules are written in concrete. I never break them, no matter how tempting the offer."

It was a gently administered rebuff and maybe if they'd been alone, Roxanne would have taken it better. Unfortunately, Catherine's presence heaped humiliation on top of embarrassment. Deciding it was time to make a tactful retreat, Catherine offered the two her most professional smile.

"If you'll excuse me," she murmured, "I'll leave you to enjoy the party while I get back to work. If there's anything I can do to make your evening more pleasant, please don't hesitate to let me know."

With that, she made a beeline for the kitchen. Damn it. Roxanne would not appreciate her witnessing that little scene with Gabe. She could only hope that by making a swift departure, she dodged any sort of bullet fired off as retribution. She couldn't afford for anything to go wrong tonight. If Gabe's precious assistant decided to even the score a little, it could cause serious trouble for Elegant Events. Catherine managed a full dozen steps before she was caught by the arm and swung around.

"You don't want to leave now," Roxanne insisted in an undertone, anchoring her in place. "The party's just about to get interesting."

Catherine's eyes narrowed. "What are you talking about?" she demanded.

Roxanne simply smiled. "Wait for it…. Ah, right on cue."

The roar of multiple engines echoed from across the lake and a pair of bullet-shaped motorboats bore down on the area reserved for the gondolas.

Three

Catherine stared in horror. "Oh, no. No, no, no."

"Now, *that* doesn't look good," Roxanne observed with a well satisfied smile. "Maybe this part of the lake wasn't the best place to put your little boats."

At the last possible instant, the invading crafts cut their engines, sending huge swells careening among the gondolas, overturning three of them and swamping most of the others. Shrieks of panic echoed across the lake as guests, dressed in their party finery, tumbled into water that still clung to its springtime chill.

While Roxanne sauntered back toward the house, Catherine yanked her walkie-talkie from a holster clipped to the belt at her waist and depressed the mike. "I need everyone out to the lake. *Now*." She ran toward the shoreline, even as she barked orders. Off to her left, she saw Gabe flying across the lawn toward the water, as well as several of the other men present. "There's been an accident with the gondolas. There are guests in the water. Everyone drop what you're doing and help. Davis…call marine patrol and have them dispatch emergency vehicles immediately."

Within minutes, guests and staff alike were pulling people from the water. "I want the gondoliers locating those guests who were in their individual boat," Catherine called out. Comprehension was instantaneous and the gondoliers immediately started rounding up and organizing their passengers to confirm that everyone who went into the lake had come safely out of it. "Make sure every guest is accounted for. Report to me as soon as you've counted heads."

Natalie appeared at her side. A combination of tears and fury burned in her eyes. "How could you let this happen?" she demanded. "My father-in-law is out there. My grandchildren are out there."

"Try and stay calm, Natalie. I'll have everyone accounted for in just a few minutes," Catherine attempted to reassure her.

"Calm! Don't tell me to be calm." She hovered along the edge of the grass, desperately scanning the crowd of soaked guests for family members. Tears fell as she spotted them. "If anything happens to my family or friends as a result of this, I will sue you six ways to Sunday!"

"I'm sorry, Natalie. Truly, I am. We've called the King County Marine Unit. They're on their way. The area is posted. I had boats anchored just outside the warning buoys to help direct lake traffic away from this section, but they simply drove straight through." She gestured toward the motorboats responsible. "If the marine unit catches these guys before they disappear, they'll take the appropriate action. In the meantime, all my staff is down there helping people ashore. We're going to need towels, if you have them."

"Of course I have towels," she snapped. "But that doesn't change what's happened. This is an unmitigated disaster. I was warned not to hire you, Catherine. But I liked you. You told me you could do the job and do it perfectly. You knew how important this was to me—"

Catherine never heard the rest of Natalie's comment, perhaps because it ended in a shriek as water seemed to explode around them. Sprinkler heads popped up across the lawn and shot drenching sprays over the guests, the tables and the food. Within seconds, those who hadn't been thrown in the lake were as thoroughly soaked as those who had been.

People fled in all directions. Natalie's daughter tripped over a peg anchoring one of the tents and knocked a billowing section into the hot dishes. The flame from the fuel canisters leapt onto the material and raced hungrily across the silk and tulle. If it hadn't been for the sprinklers, the entire area would have turned into an inferno.

Catherine ran to the tent, yanking at the burning section in an attempt to pull it to the grass and extinguish what flames the sprinklers weren't reaching. She felt the scorching heat lick at her hands. She'd barely managed to knock the awning to the ground, where the flames subsided with a smoky hiss, when an arm locked around her waist and swept her clear of the area. The next thing she knew she was tumbled to the grass and rolled repeatedly. She struggled against her attacker, even managing to connect with a fist to an iron-hard jaw before his hold loosened. Shoving her sopping hair from her face, she found herself pinned to the ground, nose-to-nose with Gabe.

Catherine fought for air while tears of outrage welled up in her eyes. "What the hell are you doing? Why did you tackle me?" She couldn't seem to make sense of what was happening. "I was trying to put out the flames."

"So was I. You were on fire, Catherine." He snagged the sleeve of her dress and showed her the scorch marks. Then he ripped the seam of her sleeve from wrist to shoulder and checked her skin for burns. He didn't find any, and an expression of undisguised relief flashed across his face. "Looks like I caught it in time. Another minute and you'd have been on your way to the hospital."

"I…I thought I was being attacked."

"So I gathered." He waggled his jaw from side to side. "That's one hell of a right hook you have, by the way."

She buried her head against his shoulder and fought for control. Everything had happened so fast, she couldn't make sense of it all. "I don't understand any of this, Gabe. The fire… Dear God, the tent went up so fast. If anyone had been nearby—"

He wrapped her in a tight embrace. "Easy, honey. Everyone's safe. And everyone made it out of the water without injury. Best of all, the marine unit has the boaters corralled."

She could feel her emotions slipping and struggled to hang on. Hysterics wouldn't help. Not here. Not now. She needed to keep a level head until she could get home and crawl into some dark hole. "Who were they?" She forced herself to pull free of Gabe's protective hold even though it would have been so much easier to cling. She fought her way to her knees. "And how did the sprinklers turn on? I checked them myself. They're not scheduled to start up until morning."

"I don't know." He soothed with both voice and touch. "Let's take everything one step at a time, sweetheart. I know it looks bad, but we'll figure out what happened and why."

She knelt there, soaked and shivering, as she scanned the area. Tables were overturned, chairs upended. Shards of shattered crystal and china glittered under the outdoor lights. The other tents had also been knocked askew by fleeing guests, though miracle of miracles, they hadn't caught fire as this one had. But the buffet tables had all tipped. Food littered the grass in soggy heaps. Along the outskirts of the property, people were milling, looking shell-shocked.

Dear heaven. Catherine bowed her head, defeat weighing heavy. "I guess I won't need your help saving my business, considering that my career is now officially over."

"Not necessarily." Compassion rippled through his voice. "I've turned around companies in worse predicaments."

For a split second she felt a resurgence of hope. She lifted her head to look at him. "Do you really think Elegant Events can recover from this?"

"We'll never know until we try."

Catherine took a deep breath. "In that case…" It would seem she only had one remaining option. "I don't suppose your offer from this morning is still on the table?"

Not a scrap of triumph showed in his voice or expression. "It was never off."

Early morning sunshine flooded Dina's kitchen and turned the glass insets of her cabinets into polished mirrors. "You don't have to do this, Catherine," Dina protested. "You don't have to acquiesce to whatever terms Gabriel foisted on you during a critical moment. Considering the circumstances—"

"Considering the circumstances, yes, I do," Catherine insisted. "I've always been a woman of my word, and that's not going to change just because I was under pressure last night. If anyone can salvage something from the Marconi disaster, it's Gabe. Trust me, we need someone of his caliber if we're going to keep Elegant Events from becoming known as Deadly Disasters."

Catherine leaned a hip against the countertop and tried not to think about the previous evening. It was bad enough that she'd spent the entire night with various highlights rampaging through her head. It was time to focus on solutions for the future, instead of dwelling on unalterable past events. But she couldn't seem to help herself. In the wee hours of the morning she'd reached a few unpleasant conclusions. Though she refused to accept blame for the boaters—that she could lay firmly at Roxanne's doorstep—the other incidents were the ones that troubled her the most.

It had been her initials on the checklist beside the detail that read "change the time on the automated sprinklers." She distinctly remembered doing so. In fact, she'd checked the digital read-out a second time before the party started, just to be certain. She tapped her fingers on the countertop. Maybe she'd made a mistake. Maybe she'd pushed p.m. instead of a.m., even though at the time she'd been very careful to avoid just such a mistake.

And then there'd been the tent peg. She couldn't blame that one on Roxanne, either. She'd seen Natalie's daughter trip over the anchor rope and uproot the peg. Granted, the wet ground might have loosened it. But it was her responsibility to make certain such incidents didn't happen. Period. That was the entire premise behind her business.

"I know what you're doing, and you have to stop it, Catherine." Dina crossed to her side and gave her a swift hug. "You're going to drive yourself into exhaustion over something that wasn't your fault, and that's not going to help. Let's deal with one issue at a time, starting with…" She pulled back. "What, exactly, did you promise Gabriel, if you don't mind my asking?"

"That I'd move in with him." Just saying the words

was hard enough. She had no idea how she'd be able to handle the reality of living with him again. "I promised I'd stay with him until he figured a way to turn Elegant Events around. Though after last night—"

"As you said yourself, if anyone can do it, it's Gabriel."

"I don't doubt he'll be able to figure out why the business is losing money."

"It is his specialty," his mother admitted. "When he took over Piretti's he nailed the financial end of our problems and plugged the leaks within a month. He's only gotten better since. He can take apart a company and put it together again better than anyone I've ever seen. He's even better at it than his father."

"That's what I'm counting on. It's our other problems that he's going to find a bit more difficult. If we can't figure out why we're unable to nail certain key contracts, how can he? And now, after the Marconi incident, that may not even matter. Somehow we're going to have to come up with a dynamite scheme to rebuild our reputation." She eyed Dina grimly. "I'm expecting a slew of cancelations the minute word gets out. And I doubt our contract is sufficiently bulletproof to keep them from walking."

"Gabriel might be able to talk them around."

"Someone better be able to."

"So what's the next step?" Dina asked. "Where do we go from here?"

Catherine rubbed at the headache pounding against her temples. "I have a meeting with Gabe in just under an hour. We're supposed to discuss strategy. I'd like you to continue to man the office, if you don't mind. You've always been incredible at sweet-talking the customers when they call."

Dina's smile flashed. "I give great phone."

For the first time in what seemed like forever, Catherine laughed. It felt wonderful, almost a purging. "Yes, you do," she agreed. "If you would do your best to give unbelievable phone today, I'd be grateful."

"Anything I can do to help. You know that."

"Yes, I do." She caught Dina's hand in hers. "How can I thank you for all you've done? Not just for today, but for every day over these past two years."

The older woman shook her head. "There's nothing to thank me for."

"Please. Let me say this." Tears filled Catherine's eyes, as unexpected as they were unwanted, no doubt the result of exhaustion. "You took me in at a time I desperately needed someone. And you took me in despite the fact that I was leaving your son. You let me live here and took care of me during those first couple of months until I felt well enough to find my own place. Not only have you been a friend, but you've been the mother I never had."

"Oh, sweetheart, now you're going to make me cry. No one should lose their mother, especially not at such a young, impressionable age. If I've been able to fill in for her, even in the smallest capacity, I'm more than happy to do it. I just wish…" She caught her lip between her teeth, her expression one of intense guilt. "I have a confession to make."

"Let me guess. You weren't being altruistic when you took me in all those months ago? You did it because you were hoping Gabe and I would eventually patch things up?"

"You knew?"

"Let's say I suspected."

"I hope you're not offended."

Catherine shook her head. "Not at all." With a small exclamation, she wrapped her arms around the woman she'd once thought would be her mother-in-law and gave her a fierce hug. "Thank you for everything. Just don't get your hopes up about me and Gabe. It's only temporary. After a few months he'll realize that my leaving two years ago was inevitable. We simply aren't right for each other."

"I'm sure that's precisely what you'll discover. And I'm so sorry you've been forced into this predicament."

"Dina?"

"Yes, dear?"

"You do realize that your kitchen cabinets have glass insets, don't you?"

"Yes. I chose them myself."

"And you also realize that in this light, the glass acts like a mirror?"

"Does it?"

"I'm afraid it does. I'd have an easier time believing you felt badly about my moving back in with Gabriel if I couldn't see you pumping your fist in the air."

"I'm not pumping my fist," Dina instantly denied. "I'm giving you a totally sympathetic, albeit enthusiastic, air pat."

"I can still see you. Now you're grinning like a maniac."

"I'm just trying to put a happy face on your moving back in with Gabriel. Inside, I'm crying for you."

Catherine pulled back. "It's temporary, Dina. We're not back together again."

Dina's smile grew wicked. "Try and tell Gabriel that and see how far it gets you."

Forty-five minutes later, Catherine swept off the elevator at Piretti's and headed for Gabe's office. She'd dressed carefully in a forest-green silk suit jacket and matching A-line skirt, completing the ensemble with a pair of mile-high heels. It was one of her favorite outfits, mainly because it served as a complementary foil to her hair and eyes. The formfitting style also made the most of her subtle curves.

She'd spent the drive into the city planning how best to handle the upcoming encounter with Roxanne in the hopes it would take her mind off a far more serious issue—her upcoming encounter with Gabe. Though she'd agreed to move in with him, she hadn't agreed to anything beyond that. Before she packed a single bag, she intended to set a few ground rules, which put her at a disadvantage right off the bat. Gabe, she reluctantly conceded, was one of the best negotiators she'd ever met and if she had any hope at all in gaining the upper hand, she'd need some leverage.

To her surprise, Roxanne was nowhere in sight. Considering how hard Gabe's assistant had worked at turning the Marconi party into a grade-A disaster, perhaps she'd taken the day off to get some much-needed rest and restock on what must be a dwindling supply of venom and spite. Well, they'd have their little chat soon enough, Catherine decided. She'd make certain of that. It wouldn't matter all that much if it waited a day or two.

The door to Gabe's office was open, and Catherine paused on the threshold. He stood in profile to her in front of a bank of windows overlooking Puget Sound and she drank in the sight while heat exploded low in her belly and fanned outward to the most inconvenient places. For a split second her vision tilted and she saw, not a captain of high finance and industry, but the captain of a pirate ship.

At some point, he'd shed his suit jacket and rolled up the sleeves of his snowy shirt, exposing the bronzed skin of his forearms. His tie had long ago been ripped from its anchor around his neck and discarded, and he'd unbuttoned his shirt, revealing the broad, powerful chest she'd so often rested her head against. With his feet planted wide and his hands fisted on his hips, all he needed was a cutlass strapped to his side to complete the image. As it was, he barked out orders with all the arrogance of a pirate. But instead of it being to a crew of scallywags, he had a wireless headset hooked over his ear.

"Tell Felder the offer is good for precisely twenty-four hours." Gabe checked his watch, which told her that those hours would be timed to the minute. "After that, I won't be interested in restructuring, let alone a buyout, regardless of how he sweetens the pot." He disconnected the call and turned to face her, not appearing the least surprised to find her standing there. "Right on time. I've always appreciated that about you, Catherine."

She waded deeper into his office. "I have a lot to do today, so I didn't see any point in wasting either of our time."

"*We* have a lot to do," he corrected. "I've rescheduled my appointments today so we can formulate a tentative game plan for Elegant Events."

She made a swift recalibration, mentally rearranging a few appointments of her own. "Thank you. I appreciate your taking the time."

"It's what we agreed to, isn't it?"

He tilted his head to one side and the sunlight made his eyes burn a blue so brilliant and iridescent, it scattered every thought but one. She was moving back in with this man. Soon she'd share his life in the most private and personal ways possible. Share his home. Share space he'd marked as his. And though he'd never come right out and said it, she didn't have a single doubt that he also expected her to share his bed.

It had seemed so natural before. Hasty breakfasts that combined food and coffee and brief, passionate kisses that would—barely—get them through the day before they were able to fall on each other again in the waning hours of the evening. Long, romantic dinners, though those became more and more rare as work intruded with increasing frequency. The heady, desperate, mind-blowing lovemaking. The simple intimacy of living with someone day in and day out. She'd experienced all that with him. Wanted it. Wanted, even more, to take their relationship to the next level. Instead, they'd been unable to sustain even that much of a connection.

How could she go back to what hadn't worked before? How could she pretend that their relationship had a snowball's chance in hell of succeeding when she knew that it didn't. What had happened in the past colored too much of the present for them to ever go back. She bit down on her lip. They couldn't even forge a new, different sort of bond. It simply had no future, only a very brief, very finite now.

"Catherine?" He stepped closer. "It is what we agreed, isn't it? My help in return for your moving back in with me?"

"Gabe—" she began.

His expression hardened. "Reneging already?"

"No. I made a promise, and I'll keep it." She met his gaze, silently willing him to change his mind, to see the impossibility of his plan ever succeeding. "But you need to understand something before we take this any further. Whatever you have planned, whatever you hope to accomplish by forcing us together again, isn't going to work. You can't force a relationship."

He smiled his angel's smile while the devil gleamed in his eyes. "And you need to understand something as well. It won't take any force. All I have to do is touch you, just as all you have to do is touch me. That's all it will take, Cate. One touch and neither of us will be able to help ourselves."

She shuddered. "Then I'll have to make certain that one touch doesn't happen."

"It's already happened. It happened the minute you set foot in my office yesterday. It happened again last night during the party. You're just not willing to admit it." He reached out and tucked a loosened lock of hair behind her ear before trailing his thumb along the curve of cheek. He'd done that last night. And just as it had last night, a shaft of fire followed in the wake of his caress, forcing her to lock her knees in place in order to remain standing. "At least, you're not willing to admit it…yet."

His touch numbed her brain, making logical thought an impossibility. It had always been that way. Even so, she fought to remember what she'd planned to say to him. "We haven't set up ground rules," she managed to protest. "We need to negotiate terms."

"The terms are already set. We live together, fully and completely, with all that suggests and implies," he stated. "Now stop delaying the inevitable and let's get to work."

She lifted an eyebrow and stepped clear of his reach. It was like stepping from the deck of a ship riding turbulent seas to the calm and safety of dry land. It only took a moment to regain her balance. "Strictly business?"

He regarded her in open amusement. "Here and now, yes." He leaned in. "But what happens tonight will have nothing to do with business."

The breath stuttered in her lungs as an image of them flashed through her mind. Naked limbs entwined. Mouths fused. Male and female melding into the most intimate of bonds. How the hell did he expect her to work with that stuck in her brain?

He must have known what she was thinking because he laughed. "Don't feel bad. You're not the only one."

"Not the only one…what?"

"Who's going to find it difficult to concentrate on business today."

"That's a first," she muttered.

His amusement faded. "Not really. It just hasn't happened for a while. Not in about twenty-three months." He took a deep breath and shoved his fingers through his hair. "If your situation weren't so serious, I'd say to hell with it and have us both blow off work."

Interesting. "What would that accomplish?"

"It would give us an opportunity to get our priorities straight," he explained. "Because this time I intend to fix what went wrong."

A deep yearning filled her at the thought, one that shocked her with its intensity. Pain followed fast on its heels. He'd waited too long to compromise. Now, when it didn't matter any longer, when regaining what they'd lost had become an impossibility, he was willing to change. "We can't afford to blow off work and you know it."

"Unfortunately, we can't, no. At least, not today. And since we can't…" And just like that he switched from lover to businessman. "Let's see what we can do to salvage Elegant Events."

It took her a moment longer to switch gears. "After last night's fiasco, I expect cancelations," she warned. "A lot of them."

"You have contracts with your clients?"

"Of course. I'm not an idiot, Gabe." She closed her eyes. "I'm sorry. That was uncalled for. Blame it on exhaustion."

He let it slide without comment. "Set up appointments with those who want to cancel. Tell them that if they'll meet with you and give you a full thirty minutes of their time, and you still can't reach an amicable agreement, then you'll happily refund their deposit."

Catherine paled. "You realize what that'll mean? We'll go under if I can't salvage more than seventy-five percent of our current bookings." She rubbed a hand across her forehead. "And even that number might be wishful thinking. It could be closer to ninety."

"I can give you a more accurate figure once I examine the accounts. Who's in charge of them?"

"My partner."

His eyes narrowed. "Ah, the mysterious co-owner. You realize you can't keep her identity hidden after last night. Schedule a meeting with her. If we're going to turn your business around, I'll need to know everything about it from the ground up. And that includes whatever you can tell me about your partner."

Catherine reluctantly nodded. "I'll arrange it. What's next?"

"Next, I called Natalie Marconi, and she agreed to see us in..." He checked his watch. "An hour and a quarter. You'll be expected to tender an abject apology." He held up a hand before she could interrupt. "I know you took care of that last night, but it needs to be done again in the cold light of day. I doubt anything we do or say will help, but—"

"But we need to try."

He picked up his tie from where he'd draped it over his desk chair. "Exactly."

She shot Gabe a keen-eyed look. "Somehow I suspect she would have refused to see me if you hadn't placed the call." She didn't wait for him to confirm what she already knew. "Just so you're aware, I plan to give her a full refund."

Snagging his suit jacket, he shrugged it on. "How bad a bite is that going to take out of your reserves?"

She didn't want to think about it. "A big one," she admitted. "Not that it matters. It has to be done."

"Agreed." A hint of sympathy colored the word. He guided her from his office out into the foyer and paused beside Roxanne's vacant desk. "Let's see if meeting with her won't help you retain a small portion of goodwill."

"Where's your assistant?" Catherine asked casually while he scribbled Roxanne a quick note. At least, she hoped the question came across as casual. Considering what she'd like to do to his precious assistant, she was lucky it didn't sound as though she was chewing nails.

"In the field. I've spent the past six months negotiating a takeover of a plant that manufactures boat engines. It'll dovetail nicely with another company I own that custom-designs yachts. Right now we outsource quite a number of components. I'd like to change that."

"So you're busily acquiring businesses that manufacture those outsourced components."

"Exactly." He propped the note on Roxanne's computer keyboard before walking with Catherine to the bank of elevators. "Roxanne is working to set up a meeting to hammer out the final details. For some reason the owner, Jack LaRue, has been dragging his feet, and I need to find out why and resolve whatever issues remain. Roxanne has a way of…" He shrugged. "Let's just say, she can motivate people to stop dragging their feet."

"Got it."

The elevator doors parted and they stepped inside. "You've never cared for her, have you?" he asked.

What was the point in lying after all this time? "No."

"Is it because she took over your job? Or is it a woman thing?"

Catherine stared straight ahead and counted to ten before responding. "Call it a clash of personalities."

"Sorry. I don't buy that. What's the real reason?"

She faced him. "The truth?"

"No, I want you to lie to me."

Catherine released her breath in a frustrated sigh. "I resented having to go through her to speak to you. I resented that she had the power to decide which of those messages she'd deliver and when she'd deliver them. I also resented the fact that she didn't just want to take over my job, she wanted to take over my place in your life. Is that reason enough?"

Four

Before Gabe could respond, the elevator doors parted and Catherine exploded from the car. Her heels beat a furious tattoo across the garage surface, a beat that echoed the anger chasing through her. She hadn't realized until then how long those words had choked her and how badly she'd wanted to speak them. But now that she had, she realized they wouldn't make the least difference. He wouldn't believe her now any more than he had two years ago. When it came to Roxanne, he was as blind to her true nature as every other man.

Catherine paused beside Gabe's Jag and struggled to regain her self-control. How the hell did Roxanne do it? It wasn't just her looks. Plenty of women had incredible bodies, as well as faces that could have graced a goddess. Maybe it was the body combined with a Machia-vellian brain that would have done Lucretia Borgia proud that gave Roxanne such an edge.

Gabe opened the car door and waited while Cath-erine slid in before circling the car and climbing behind the wheel. Instead of igniting the powerful engine, he swiveled to face her. "I'm sorry. I had no idea she was such a problem for you."

"She isn't a problem. Not any longer."

"And I'll make certain of that. When you call, I'll give her strict instructions to put you straight through, even if I'm in a meeting."

"You don't have to do that."

"Yes, I do."

It took Catherine a moment to steady her breathing. "Why, Gabe?" she whispered. "Why couldn't you have done this before when it first came up? Why now when it's far too late?"

His jaw firmed, taking on an all-too familiar stubborn slant. "It's not too late." He started the engine with a roar. "You walked out on me for good cause. I admit there were problems. Serious problems. This time around, I intend to fix them."

The drive to the Marconi estate took just under an hour. A maid, all starched and formal, escorted them to an equally starched and formal parlor that overlooked the scene of last night's disaster. Catherine didn't doubt for a moment that the uncomfortable choice of venue was deliberate.

"I'm not quite sure why you're here," Natalie said,

once they were seated. She made a point of not offering them refreshments by pouring herself a cup of coffee from the gleaming silver service on the table at her side and taking a slow, deliberate sip. Her coldly furious eyes moved from Catherine to Gabe and back again. "I'm particularly in the dark about your presence, Gabe. It's Ms. Haile who owes me both an explanation and an apology."

"You're absolutely right, Mrs. Marconi." Catherine spoke up before Gabe could. "I do owe you an apology, and I can't begin to express how sorry I am that your party was ruined." She opened her purse, removed a check and placed it on the delicate coffee table that served as a buffer between her chair and Natalie's. "This is a full refund."

Twin spots of color chased across Natalie's cheekbones. "You think throwing money at me is going to fix this?"

"Not at all. I think refunding your money is the least I can do to compensate for my part in what happened. I'm sorry the security detail I hired was unable to intercept the intruders. I contacted the authorities this morning, and they informed me that the young men on the boats received an invitation from an unidentified woman. They're continuing to look into it in the hopes of pinning down precisely who extended the invite, in case you wish to pursue the matter. The boaters involved have volunteered to recompense your guests, as well as the gondola company, for any damages incurred."

"That will certainly help," she reluctantly admitted.

"And the sprinklers? That mistake is one hundred percent your fault."

Catherine inclined her head. "I accept full responsibility for that. I promise you, I double-checked to make sure they'd been disengaged for the evening. I can't explain how they were switched back on."

"I can. You're incompetent."

"Natalie," Gabe said softly.

"Well, what other explanation is there?" she retorted defensively.

"I can think of three. One, there was a power interruption and the device returned to its default setting. Two, someone accidentally changed the time. Or three, someone did it deliberately as a prank." He paused to allow that to sink in. "There were a lot of youngsters there last night who might have considered it quite a lark to have the sprinklers go on in the middle of the party and watch the mayhem from a safe distance."

Natalie sat up straighter, her eyes flashing. "Are you accusing someone in my family?"

"I'm not the one making accusations." He let that hang. "I'm simply pointing out that there are alternative explanations."

"Catherine's initials were on the checklist as the one responsible for resetting the sprinklers. I saw them there myself."

"Which means she did reset them. Why else would she have initialed it? Twice, I might add." Natalie fell silent at the sheer logic of his question. He pressed home his advantage. "You'd have more cause to point fingers if it hadn't been checked off because then you'd know she'd overlooked it."

Natalie dismissed that with a wave of her hand. "And the tent going up in flames? We could have lost our house. People could have been seriously injured, or worse."

"Your daughter tripped over the line anchoring that corner of the tent. I saw it happen. I'm sure if you ask her, she'll admit as much, especially since she twisted her ankle as a result and your son-in-law had to carry her to safety. There is no negligence here, Natalie. It was a simple, unforeseeable accident."

"On the other hand," Catherine inserted, "the point of hiring an event planner is to foresee the unforeseeable and take precautions."

Gabe turned on her. "In hindsight, what could you have done differently to prevent those accidents from happening? You'd already checked the sprinkler system. Twice. That section of the lake was posted and patrolled. And the tent was securely anchored."

Natalie released her breath in a sigh. "All right, all right. You've made your point, Gabe. I don't see how Catherine could have possibly foreseen any of those eventualities. I wish she could have, but I like to consider myself an honest and fair woman. And honesty and fairness compel me to admit that no one could have anticipated such a bizarre string of events." She looked at Catherine, this time without the anger coloring her expression. "Thank you for returning my fee and for your apology. Up until all hell broke loose, the event was brilliantly planned and executed."

Catherine stood. "I appreciate your understanding. I'd say I look forward to doing business with you at some point in the future…" She offered a self-deprecating smile. "But I have a feeling I might find a cup of that lovely coffee poured over my head."

Natalie managed a smile as well. "Good try, my dear, but there's little to no chance of my being quite that forgiving."

Catherine shrugged. "It was worth a try." She held out a hand. "Thank you for taking the time to see me."

"You can thank Gabe for that. I'm not sure I would have agreed if not for him." Her gaze swept over him, filled with pure feminine appreciation. "For some strange reason, it's impossible to say no to the man."

Catherine released a sigh of exasperation. "So, I've discovered," she murmured.

After leaving the Marconi residence, Gabe handed Catherine a business card for a transportation firm, along with the key to his apartment. "I've made arrangements with this company to move your belongings over to my place. Just call them when you're ready."

"I won't have that much," she protested, as they headed back toward the city. "Just a couple of suitcases."

He pulled onto the floating bridge that spanned Lake Washington and negotiated smoothly around oncoming traffic. "I want you to feel like you live there, not like you're a temporary guest."

"I am a temporary guest," she retorted. "The only one who doesn't realize that is you."

He didn't bother to argue. But when he pulled up in front of her apartment complex, he parked the car and exited at the same time Catherine did. He followed her across the sidewalk and up the stairs leading to the vestibule.

"You don't need to come in," she informed him over her shoulder. "I'll call the moving company if that will satisfy you."

One look at his set face warned that she wouldn't get rid of him that easily. "You'd rather have this discussion out here on a public street?" he asked with painful politeness.

"In all honesty, I'd rather not have this discussion at all," she replied.

"I'm afraid that's not one of the options available to you."

She hated when he donned his business persona. There was no opposing him. "I've agreed to your terms. What more do you want?" He simply stood and stared, and she released her breath in an irritated rush. "Fine. Let's go inside."

She led the way, choosing to take the steps to her second-floor apartment, rather than the elevator. She paused at the appropriate door and unlocked it. "Would you like a cup of the coffee Natalie didn't offer us before you leave?"

He lifted an eyebrow. "Here's your hat, what's your hurry?"

Her mouth quivered in amusement. "Something like that."

"No, what I want is to clarify a few things." He paced through the confines of her tiny living area, studying first the view, and then her furnishings. "Cozy."

"I don't require a lot of space." She dropped her keys in a green blown-glass bowl on a table near the front door. "Probably because I don't take up anywhere near as much room as you."

He turned. "Sometimes I forget how small you are. It must have something to do with that strong, passionate personality of yours."

The compliment knocked her off-kilter, and she didn't want to be off-kilter. She folded her arms across her chest. "Do you really think it's going to make the least difference to our relationship whether I move two suitcases' worth of possessions into your place or two truckloads? Possessions won't keep me there. Not when our relationship falls apart again."

He ignored that final barbed shot. "Having personal possessions around you will make you feel more comfortable. And maybe if you're more comfortable, you'll be more inclined to work through our difficulties rather than run from them."

"I didn't run the first time, Gabe."

His jaw tightened. "Didn't you? It looked like running to me. It felt like it. One minute you were there and the next you were gone. No warning. Not even a phone call."

"I left a note," she retorted, stung.

"I remember." He stalked closer. "I got home after forty-eight straight hours of a brutal work crisis that could have meant the end of Piretti's and found it waiting for me."

"What do you mean…that could have meant the end of Piretti's?" she asked in alarm. "I thought it was one of your takeovers on the verge of imploding."

"No, it was an attempted coup staged by Piretti's former board members, the ones I'd kicked out after staging my own coup. Not that it matters." He returned to his point with dogged determination. "What you did was cold, Catherine."

"You're right, it was," she conceded. "And I'm sorry for that. Someday ask me about the brutal forty-eight hours I experienced leading up to that decision. It was cold because I was cold. Cold and empty and—" She stemmed the flow of words before she said too much. She wouldn't go there with him. Didn't have the emotional stamina, even now. Even after nearly two years, she couldn't face the memories with anything approaching equanimity.

"And what? You were cold and empty and…what?" he pressed.

"Broken. Sick and broken."

She forced the words out, then busied herself opening her briefcase and removing the file on Elegant Events that she'd offered Gabe the day before. His hand dropped over hers, forcing her to set the papers aside.

"Is that why you went to stay with my mother? Because you were sick and broken?"

"I didn't have any other family," she whispered. "I didn't have anywhere else to—"

His grip gentled. "You don't have to justify it. I'm relieved that you felt comfortable going to her."

"Really?" She searched his expression, seeking reassurance. "I'm surprised you didn't give her a hard time about taking me in."

His head jerked as though she'd slapped him. "Was I such a bastard that you think I'd do such a thing to you? I'm relieved to know you had a place. To know you were safe." Then he asked the one question she dreaded most. "You said you were sick. What was wrong with you?"

"Nothing that a little tender loving care couldn't cure."

"Care I didn't offer you."

She met his gaze dead-on. "No, you didn't."

"That's going to change." He waved aside her incipient response. "I know you don't believe me. Only time will convince you otherwise, and I'm hoping the next few months will do just that."

There was no point arguing, not when he was right. Only time would give them the proof they needed…proof that they *didn't* belong together. "Fair enough."

"Call the number on the business card, Catherine," he urged. "They've been paid regardless of how much or how little you bring. And all you have to do is point out the things you want transferred. They'll pack, load and transport, and then reverse the process once they get everything over to my place."

"Thank you," she said with in a stiff voice. "That's very generous of you."

He frowned. "Don't. Please, don't."

She closed her eyes for an instant. "I'm sorry. We've

been apart so long, and—" She shook her head in bewilderment. "I don't know how to handle this."

"Then I'll show you how to handle it. It's easy." He cupped her face and feathered a kiss across her mouth. It was soft and gentle and drove every ounce of common sense straight out of her head. "See how easy?"

"I still don't—"

She never completed the sentence. She never even completed the thought. It faded away, forever lost. His mouth returned to hers, and the tenor of the kiss changed, grew more potent. He slipped a small demand into the embrace, urging a response she was helpless to resist. So she didn't resist. After that it seemed such a small step to go from reluctant response to active participation. To meet his demand and make one of her own. To give. To take. To nudge up the heat ever so slightly.

She felt the tilt, the inner shift from submission to aggression. She slid her arms across his chest and shoved at his suit jacket. She caught the whisper of silk as it slipped away. Not breaking contact, she yanked his tie from its mooring, ripping at the knot until it followed the same path as his jacket. Plucking at the buttons of his shirt, she finally, *finally,* hit hot, firm flesh.

Heaven help her, but he was built. Her mouth slid from his and traced a pathway along his corded throat and downward. She felt the groan vibrating beneath her lips and smiled. She remembered that sound, the pleasure it gave her to be the cause. To thrill at the knowledge that her touch could drive a man of Gabe's strength of will to lose total control.

Even now she felt him teetering on the brink and caught herself hovering there as well. She had just enough awareness to realize she had a choice. She could finish what she'd started, or she could pull back. Part of her, the part that longed to feel Gabe's hands on her again and experience anew that incredible rush when their bodies joined, urged her to continue. But there were too many issues between them for her to give in so quickly and easily.

As though sensing her hesitation, he gave a push of his own. "I've missed you, Catherine," he murmured roughly. He followed the tailored line of her suit, reacquainting himself with familiar territory. Fire splashed in the wake of his touch. "And I've missed this."

She wouldn't be able to hold out much longer. It was now or never. With a reluctant sigh, she pulled back and felt the first tiny shudder of her common sense returning. "You don't fight fair," she complained. She gave his chest a final nipping kiss and stepped clear of his embrace. "I guess you think this proves your point."

"If I could remember what the hell my point was, I'd agree with you. But since every ounce of blood has drained from my head to places lacking brain cells, I don't think that's going to happen." He lifted a sooty eyebrow. "I don't suppose you remember what my point was?"

"Can't say that I do."

He grinned. "Liar."

She cleared her throat. "It might have been that living together again will be like riding a bicycle. Once we start pedaling, the moves will come back to us."

"I have to admit, I don't remember that part of our conversation, but it sounds good to me." His eyes sharpened, the blue growing more intense. "The business card. The movers. Your doubts."

She smiled with something approaching affection. "Ah, there he is. Back to business-as-usual."

His mouth twitched in an answering smile. Not that it kept him from staying on target this time round. "How about this. Have the movers take less than I'm asking and more than you want. Is that a reasonable compromise?"

"Yes."

"Does that mean yes, you'll do it?"

She nodded. "I should be there well before dinnertime."

Satisfaction settled over him. "Perfect. I've arranged for something special for tonight." He tapped the tip of her nose with his index finger. "And no, I didn't mean anything sexual, so don't go all indignant on me."

"Hmm." She tilted her head to one side and scrutinized him through narrowed eyes. "Despite your assurances, I somehow suspect you'll get there later, if not sooner."

"You can count on it." The promise glittered like sapphires in his gaze and gave the hard angle of his jaw an uncompromising set. "But in this case I was actually talking about dinner."

"You don't have to do anything special," she protested.

He hooked her chin with his knuckle so they were eye-to-eye. "Yes," he assured her. "I do. I'll see you about six."

The rest of the day flew by. Giving in to the inevitable, she phoned the movers. She barely hung up the phone before two burly men arrived on her doorstep. It was almost as easy as shopping on the Internet. They were user-friendly, and all she had to do was point and click. In no time they had far too many of her possessions packed and carted down to their moving truck. Just as Gabe predicted, the other end of the procedure proved equally as painless.

The one uncomfortable moment came when they asked where they should put her clothing. She briefly debated whether to direct them to one of the spare bedrooms, or to Gabe's master suite. Considering the close call she and Gabe had experienced back at her apartment, it seemed pointless to take a stand she suspected wouldn't last more than a single night. Even though she knew that nothing would come of their relationship—that nothing *could* come of it—she might as well enjoy the fantasy while it lasted.

The instant the door closed behind the movers, she finished the few unpacking chores she preferred to see to herself. Then she took a leisurely tour of Gabe's penthouse suite. It felt peculiar to be back again. Part of her felt right at home, as though she'd never left.

There was the table where she used to sit and keep track of their social calendar and plan the parties that had become her specialty. And in the window seat over there, she and Gabe would curl up together on a quiet Sunday morning over a steaming cup of coffee while they watched the rain pound the city. And over there... How many times had they entertained guests in the living room? Gabe would sit in that enormous chair he'd had specially designed, and she'd squeeze into a corner next to him.

Of course, there were a few changes. A different set of throw pillows were scattered on the sofa. She came across a gorgeous wooden sculpture that hadn't been there before. It was of a woman in repose and made her itch to run her fingertips along the graceful, sweeping lines. The drapes were new, as were a pair of planters on either side of the front door.

After delaying the inevitable as long as she could, she gathered her nerve and entered the bedroom, only to discover this room showed the most changes of all. The previous bed and furniture, darkly masculine pieces, had been removed, and Gabe had replaced them with furnishings made with a golden teak heartwood that brought to mind sailing ships from the previous century. Catherine couldn't help but smile. Nothing could have suited him better, though she couldn't help but wonder why he'd replaced his previous bedroom set.

To her surprise, the changes brought her a sense of relief, as though all the old, negative energy had been swept clean. Checking her watch, she realized that Gabe would be home in just under an hour and if he'd planned something special for their dinner, maybe she should consider dressing for the occasion.

She took her time primping, finally settling on a casual floor-length sheath in an eye-catching turquoise. For the first time in ages, she left her hair loose and flowing, a tidal wave of springy curls that tumbled down her back in reckless abandon. She touched up her makeup, giving her eyes and mouth a bit more emphasis.

She'd just finished when the doorbell rang, and she went to answer it, fairly certain it was whatever dinner surprise Gabe had arranged. Sure enough, it proved to be a small catering company that she'd used for a few of her events. She greeted the chef by name and showed her and her companion to the kitchen.

"Gabe said we were to get here right at six and serve no later than six-thirty," Sylvia explained. "It'll only take a few minutes to unload the appetizers and get them heated. In the meantime, I'll open the wine and let it breathe while Casey sets the dining room table. She'll be serving you tonight."

"Thanks," Catherine said with a warm smile. "I'll be in the living room. Gabe should be home any minute."

Or so she thought. By six-thirty, she'd nibbled her way through any number of appetizers that she was certain should have tasted like ambrosia, but for some reason had the flavor and consistency of sawdust. At a quarter to seven Sylvia appeared in the doorway. "Should I hold dinner a little longer? I'm afraid to wait too long or it'll be overcooked."

"Hold off for fifteen more minutes. If he's not here by then, you can wrap everything up and stash it in the fridge."

"Oh. Oh, sure. We can do that."

Catherine flinched at the unmistakable pity in the other woman's voice. "Thanks, Sylvia. I'll be in the bedroom if you need me."

Keeping her chin high, she marched to the master

suite and gently closed the door. Then she proceeded to remove her belongings and transfer them to one of the guest bedrooms. Why, oh why, had she allowed herself to believe for even one single second that he'd changed? Nothing had changed. Business always came first with Gabe and it always would.

From deep inside the apartment the phone rang. More than anything, she wanted to ignore it. But it would only make matters worse if she allowed the answering machine to take the call so that Sylvia and Casey could overhear whatever excuse Gabe cared to offer for his delay.

She picked up the bedroom extension. "Hello?"

"I'm sorry." Gabe's voice rumbled across the line. "This wasn't how I planned our first night together."

She held on to her self-control by a shred. "I'm sure it wasn't."

"You're furious, and I don't blame you. That deal I told you about earlier came to a head. Roxanne managed to get LaRue to the table, and this was the only time he'd agree to."

"I'll bet."

"It's going to be a while. I'll be home as soon as I can."

She heard the unspoken question and answered it. "I promised I'd be here, and I will. The rest we'll negotiate in the morning."

He swore softly. "This will be the last time."

She shook her head in disbelief. He still didn't get it. "You think it will, Gabe. That's part of the problem. You always think that next time will be different. But it never is, is it?"

She didn't wait for his response, but hung up. She needed to inform the caterers that their services wouldn't be required. But first, she needed a moment to herself. A moment to grieve over the death of a tiny blossom of hope that had somehow, at some point when she wasn't looking, managed to unfurl deep in her heart.

Five

It was two in the morning before Gabe keyed open the lock to his apartment. Catherine had left a light burning for him, the one by the sculpture of the sleeping woman—a sculpture whose gentle curves and sleek, soft lines reminded him vividly of her. It was why he'd bought the damn thing, even though he suspected it would torment him every time he looked at it. And it did.

Turning off the light, he headed directly for the bedroom, pulling up short when he realized Catherine wasn't there. For a single, hideous moment, he flashed back on the night she'd left him. His gaze shot to the dresser, half expecting to see another crisp white envelope with his name neatly scripted across the front. Of course, it wasn't there. Nor was the dresser. Within a week of her departure, memories too painful to bear had him replacing every stick of furniture in the room.

Stripping off his suit jacket and tie, he went in search of Catherine. He found her in the spare bedroom farthest from the master suite. She sat at a small antique desk by the window, her head pillowed in her arms, sound asleep. She wore a long, sweeping silk nightgown in a stunning shade of aqua, covered by a matching robe.

Gabe silently approached and glanced at the papers littering the desk beneath and around her. They were accounting records, he realized, and he tugged free a few of the sheets. As he glanced down the rows and across the columns, a frown knit his brow. Hell, she was skating precariously close to disaster. First thing tomorrow, he'd take a closer look at this and see just how close to the edge she'd come and what it would take to turn it around…assuming that was even possible.

Tossing the pages aside, he circled the desk and gently tipped her out of the chair and into his arms. She stirred within his hold, but didn't awaken until he reached their bedroom and eased her onto the bed. She stared up at him in confusion, her golden eyes heavy with exhaustion and brimming with vulnerability.

"What…?"

"You fell asleep at your desk."

He saw the instant her memory snapped back into place, watching with keen regret as her defenses came slamming down. She bolted upright. "What am I doing in your bed? How did I get here?" she demanded.

"You're in my bed because it's where you belong,"

he explained calmly. "And you got here because I carried you here."

"Well, you can just carry me back, because I'm not staying."

He toed off his shoes without saying a word. Then he proceeded to strip. He was one article of clothing away from baring it all when she erupted off the bed.

"You're not listening, Gabe. I'm not sleeping with you."

"Then don't sleep," he retorted mildly. "But when we go to bed, we'll be doing it together."

She shook her head, and her sleep-tangled curls danced in agitation. "You stood me up tonight. You promised me this time would be different and then you stood me up." The vulnerability he'd seen earlier leaked through her defenses, nearly killing him. "You can't do that and then expect me to—" She waved a hand in the direction of the bed.

"Just for my own edification, is this how I'm supposed to react when the shoe is on the other foot?" he asked.

That stopped her, if only for a moment. "What do you mean?"

"I mean that your business is as demanding as mine. Most of your events take place in the evening or on the weekend when I'm off work. Having spent the past two years building up your business, you know there are times when the unexpected arises and you have no choice but to deal with it."

"Damn you!" She glared at him in frustration. "I'm not in the mood for your brand of logic. You can't turn this back on me."

"I'm not trying to. I'm trying to make you see that every once in a while something like this is going to happen. We'd better learn to deal with it starting right here and right now. Tonight was on me, and I'm sorry, Cate. I'm more sorry than you can possibly know. I wanted your homecoming to be special, and instead it was a nightmare. But you tell me how to handle it the next time or how I should react when you're the one calling with the last-minute emergency."

He could tell she was at a loss for words. The fire died, leaving behind pain and confusion. "I was looking forward to tonight so much," she confessed.

The admission hit and hit hard. "So was I." He stripped off his shorts and tossed back the bedcovers. Then he held out his hand. "Robe."

When she didn't immediately comply, he simply took matters into his own hands. He flicked buttons through holes with ruthless efficiency before sweeping it from her shoulders.

"Don't," she whispered. "Please don't."

If she'd used anger against him, or that ice-cold wall of defiance, he might have ignored her request. But he couldn't resist her when every scrap of defensive armor lay shattered around her and unhappiness coursed from her in palpable waves.

"Okay, sweetheart," he said in a husky voice. "It's okay. We'll just sleep."

He gathered her close, locking her against him, and his eyes shut at the feel of her body curving into his. This time she didn't protest when he urged her toward the bed. How long had it been since he'd had her head pillowed on his shoulder and felt those crisp, wayward curls tickle his jaw? How long had he waited to have that silken skin flowing over his, her small, perfect breasts pressed against his side? He'd craved this, just this, for endless, torturous months. Now that he had her back in his arms he could afford to be patient. As much as he wanted to make love to her, this would do until the time was right. He could give her some space while they worked through their issues.

"Are you asleep?" she asked.

"Not yet."

"Did you make the deal?"

He smiled. It was a start. He could be satisfied with that.

Gabe woke at first light and realized that this time he wasn't dreaming. This time it was real. He held Catherine safely tucked within his arms, tight against his side, the rhythm of her heart and breath and sleep-laden movements perfectly synchronized with his. He'd always considered her an elegant woman, small and delicate. But not here. Not now. Not when she abandoned herself to sleep and was at her most unguarded. Then he saw through all the defenses and shields to the very core of the woman. Mysterious. Powerful. Gloriously female.

She'd entwined her body around his, all slender shapely arms and legs. Even in sleep she clung to him, a delicious, possessive hold that cut through all the conflicts and difficulties that separated them and simply lay claim. In the real world she dressed with style, presented herself with calm self-confidence. She'd always impressed him with her cool, professional demeanor. But here in their bed she revealed a passion that never failed to set him on fire.

He traced the planes of her face, reveling in the sensation of warm, silken skin, skin covering a bone structure of such purity that it quickened his breath and annihilated reason. He thought he would forgot, that over the long months they were apart that time would steal precious memories. But it didn't. He knew each curve, remembered them all, would have recognized the feel of her, even if he'd been blind.

She was back. Granted, it wasn't out of choice. But in time, that would change. He'd make sure of it. His fingers trailed downward, across a pale shoulder, sculpting the feminine dip and swell of waist and hip. The hem of her nightgown had bunched high on her slender thighs, offering him a tantalizing view of the shapely curve of her backside. He'd missed waking up to this. Would she still moan if he caressed those sinewy lines with his fingertips?

He put thought into action and was rewarded with the lightest of sighs, one of undeniable pleasure. She shifted against him, softening and opening. Her head tipped back, spilling golden curls across their pillow, offering up the long sweep of her throat. He buried his mouth against the hollow at the very base and at the same time cupped her breast through the thin layer of silk covering it. It felt warm within his palm, the nipple a small perfect bud, ripe for the plucking. He grazed the tip. Once. Twice. The third stroke had her stirring with his name on her lips, the sound escaping in a strangled cry of sheer need.

There wasn't any just-woke-up confusion about Catherine. There never had been. She went from a dead sleep to aroused woman in the blink of an eye. Her arms circled his neck and she pulled him in for a hot, hungry kiss. He didn't need further prompting. He rolled over on top of her, sinking into her warmth.

He'd planned to give her a moment to adjust to both his weight and his embrace. But she took the initiative. Hooking a leg around his waist, she anchored him close and deepened the kiss. In this area they'd always been in perfect accord, each the perfect mate for the other. Her lips parted and he delved inward, stoking the heat. He could feel her tremble in response to his touch, feel her heartbeat pounding against his palm, and his own pulse caught the rapid-fire rhythm and echoed it.

Need ripened between them, escalating with dizzying speed. As though sensing it, she ended the kiss with a small, nipping tug of his bottom lip. "Not so fast." The request was half plea, half demand. "Give me time to think."

"Forget it, Catherine. No more waiting. This is all that matters," he told her fiercely. Once again he plied her lips with small, biting kisses while his hands traversed sweetly familiar pathways that had been left unexplored for far too long. "This is what's important. What we feel right here and right now."

"I wish that were true." Her breath hitched when he reacquainted himself with a particularly vulnerable curve of skin, just along the outer swell of her breast. "But we can't just forget what came before. What about my reasons for leaving you? What about all the empty space during the time we were apart? As enjoyable as it will be, knotting up the bedsheets isn't going to make all our problems go away."

"But it'll ground us," he maintained. "It'll give us a common base from which to work." He swept his hand across her heated flesh to prove his point, watching as her eyes glazed and her breath exploded. "We were meant to be together."

She managed to shake her head, but he could see the effort it took her. If he pressed, she'd cave. And though parts of him wanted her any way he could have her, the rational part of his brain preferred her willing, not fighting regrets. He leaned in and gave her another wickedly slow, thorough kiss before easing back.

She eyed him in open suspicion, while she probed her swollen lips with the tip of her tongue. "Are they smoking? They feel like they're smoking."

He choked on a laugh. How did she do it? How did she take him from overwhelming hunger to heart-melting amusement with one simple question? "Your lips aren't smoking, but your tongue is. Just a little around the edges." He leaned in. "I can show you where. Make it all better."

Now it was her turn to laugh. "I'll just bet." She closed her eyes. "You make it impossible to think."

"Then don't." He couldn't keep his hands off her. "Just feel."

"That's not smart. Nor is it safe."

"I won't hurt you, Cate."

He felt the tremor that shook her, the quiver of re-membered pain. "You already have," she whispered.

"Let me heal some of that hurt."

His offer provoked tears and they glittered in her eyes like gold dust. He didn't know if he'd said the right thing, or the wrong. He just knew it was honest, welling from the very core of him. Her arms slid up along his chest in response and she cupped his face. This time she initiated the embrace. It was her lips that sought his and slid like a quiet balm over his mouth. She probed with a delicacy unique to her, dancing lightly. Sweetly. Tenderly.

Just as he'd reacquainted himself with the dip and swell, the remarkable texture and scent, now so did she. Her hands cruised along his back, testing far harder planes and angles than those he'd examined. "This is where you carry it," she told him between kisses. "The weight of your responsibilities."

He trailed his fingers along her shoulders, scooping up the narrow straps of her nightgown and teasing them down her arms. "I'm strong. I can take a lot of weight."

"Not right now. Right now I want you right here. With me. No responsibilities. No interruptions. Just the two of us."

Didn't she understand? "There's nowhere else for me to be." And he'd find a way to prove it.

He painted a series of kisses along the lacy edge of

her nightgown where it dipped low over her breasts, and nudged the flimsy barrier from his path. He nearly groaned at the feel of satiny skin against his mouth and cheek. Her breasts were glorious, small, firm, and beautifully shaped, but then so was she. He caught her nipple between his teeth and tugged ever so gently, watching the wash of color that blossomed across her skin and turned her face a delicate shade of rose.

"Your eyes have gone dark," he told her. "Like antique gold."

"They haven't gone dark." Her breath escaped in a wispy groan. "They've gone blind."

"You don't need to see. Just feel."

More than anything, he wanted to make this perfect for her. To heal some of what had gone before. As much as he wanted to take her, to bury himself in her warmth and create that ultimate joining, this first time would be for her. He'd give her slow. He'd give her gentle. And he'd give her the healing she so desperately craved.

He danced with her, danced with mouth and hands and quiet caresses, driving her ever higher toward that elusive pinnacle. The air grew thick and heavy with need, tightening around them until all that existed was man and woman and the desire that bound two into one. He drove her, ever upward, knowing just how to touch, just where to stroke until her muscles clenched and she hovered on the crest.

And then he mated their bodies, kissing away the helpless tears that clung to her lashes like a dusting of diamonds. Slow and easy he moved, sliding her up and up and up, before tipping her over and tumbling down the other side with her. For a long time afterward they clung to each other, wrapped together in a slick tangle of limp arms and legs.

"I can't remember how to breathe," he managed to say.

"Funny. I can't remember how to move." She opened a single eye. "If I breathe for you, can you move for me?"

"I'll get right on that." He groaned. "Tomorrow, maybe."

"Okay." She fell silent for so long he thought she'd gone back to sleep. Then she asked, "Why, Gabe?"

"Why, what?" he asked lazily.

She opened her eyes, eyes clear and bright and glittering like the sun. "You were always a generous lover. But this morning… This morning was a gift."

He grinned. "Then just accept it and say thank you."

"Thank you."

"You're welcome."

"It makes me wonder, though…" A small frown creased her brow, like a thundercloud creeping over the horizon. "Where do we go from here? What do you want from me?"

He answered honestly. "Whatever you're willing to give."

She absorbed that, turned it over in her mind, before nodding. "That's easy enough. I can't give you permanent, but I can give you temporary. We can enjoy each other these next few months. I don't have a problem with that."

His jaw tightened. "And then?"

Something about her easy smile rang false. "Then we go our separate ways, of course. We tried living together once. It didn't work, remember?"

How could she lie beneath him and act as though what they felt was transient? Didn't she feel the connection, the way their bodies fused one to the other? The way their minds and spirits were so evenly matched? "What if a couple months isn't enough?" he argued. "It wasn't last time."

He watched her pick and choose her words and his suspicion grew. She was hiding something, keeping a part of herself locked carefully away. "We were different people then. We had different goals in life. You wanted a woman who would take care of the social end of your life. Someone who would nurture you and your home. At the time, I thought that would be enough to satisfy me, too."

"Is this about your career?" Relief swept through him and he almost laughed. "You think I object to you running your own business?"

"No...at least, not yet. But I have a feeling the time will come when you'd expect me to set it aside in order to fulfill more pressing obligations."

"More pressing obligations," he repeated. His eyes narrowed. "Are you talking about children?"

She refused to meet his eyes. "I don't want children, Gabe. I want a career. You made it crystal clear to me before I left that you were planning on a large family, just like the one you had growing up."

He sat up and thrust a hand through his hair. "Is that

why you left?" he demanded in disbelief. "Because you didn't want to have a baby?"

"You were pressing for one."

"Damn it, I asked you to marry me."

"I remember," she retorted. "It was a beautiful proposal...right up until work reared its ugly head. Roxanne's call cut me off midsentence, do you even remember that?"

He fought to recall. She'd been crying. They'd been tears of joy, of that he was certain. She'd been shaking and laughing while those tears had slid down her face. And she'd said something.... Hell. What had it been? "You had something you wanted to tell me." He shrugged. "I assume it was, 'Yes, darling, I'll marry you.' Or did I get even that wrong?"

"It doesn't matter, anymore, does it? Because you left." She spoke carefully, as though holding those long-ago emotions at a cautious distance. "You left me there with the beautiful flowers and an uneaten dinner congealing on the plate. You left me with your gorgeous ring and empty promises echoing in my ear. Because when it came right down to it, your top priority was and always will be Piretti's. So you left, explaining without saying a word where our relationship rated in the grand scheme of things, and you didn't come home again. Not that day. And not the next."

"Hell, Catherine. You may not have known about the attempted takeover two years ago, but I explained all this to you yesterday at your apartment. What was I supposed to do? Let Piretti's go under? Let those bastards take my business from me?" He stood and yanked on his clothes. "And I did come home. I came home to find a stilted little note from you and the ring you'd cried such pretty tears over sitting on my damned dresser."

If nothing else, their lovemaking had opened a wide crack in her defenses, allowing him to see all she'd kept buried before. And what he saw was pain and fear and vulnerability. "Why would you expect anything else, Gabe? Do you think I'm some sort of plaything that you can pick up and discard when it suits you? Did you ever wonder what I did while you were off running your empire? Or did you simply stick me on a shelf and forget about me until it was time to come home and pick me up again? I don't go into hibernation like one of your damn computers."

"I never said—" He thrust a hand through his hair and blew out his breath, fighting for calm. "Is there a reason we're dredging all this up again? I know what happened. And I know that you wanted more from our relationship than I could give you before. I'm willing to do that. But I don't see the point in rehashing the past."

"If not now, then when?" She tilted her head to one side. "Or were you hoping it no longer matters and move on?"

"You're good at pointing the finger, Catherine. And I'm being as honest as I know how. I screwed up. I made mistakes. But if we're going to go there and dig into all that muck, then you have to be honest, too."

Her eyes widened. "Meaning?"

"Meaning... I'm willing to continue this conversation when you stop lying and tell me what really happened. Why did you really leave me?"

She shook her head in instant denial. "I don't know what you're—"

"Bull. Just cut the bull, will you?"

He snatched a deep breath and fought for control. For some reason his gaze landed on the bedside table. A cell phone sat there, not his. He eyed it for a long minute as he considered how and when Catherine had left it there. And then he knew. She hadn't taken the bedroom at the end of the hallway when she'd moved in the previous day. She'd moved her things in here with him, at least initially. He could make a pretty accurate guess when that had changed and why. Crossing the room, he picked up the phone and tossed it to her.

"Call your partner," he instructed. "Have her meet us at Piretti's in an hour."

"Excuse me? We were in the middle of a—"

"An argument?" he shot at her.

"A discussion."

Right. "Well, it's one we're going to set aside until you come clean. Until then, it's off the table."

Indignation shot across her face and reverberated in her voice. "Just like that?"

He inclined his head. "Just like that." He deliberately changed the subject. "I saw some of your financial records last night. And I did a quick scan of the documents you provided when I returned to the office yesterday. You told me your partner handles the books?"

"Yes, but—"

"Then I want to meet her. Now." She opened her mouth to argue again, and he cut her off without compunction. "You came to me for help," he reminded her. "This is how I help."

"Okay, fine. I'll call her."

"I'm going to shower. You're welcome to join me."

"Another time, perhaps."

He managed a smile. "I'll hold you to that." He started toward the bathroom, then paused. "The breakup in our relationship? It wasn't about children or careers, Catherine. There's something else going on. I just haven't figured out what, yet. But I will. And when I do, we'll do more than put it back on the table. We're going to have this out, once and for all."

Six

They accomplished the brief ride from the apartment to Piretti's in silence. Catherine appeared a little paler than Gabe liked, but whether it was the result of the upcoming meeting with her partner, or because of their argument, he wasn't certain. Perhaps a bit of both.

Roxanne was already at her desk when they arrived, and he watched with interest as the two women exchanged a long look. Another brewing problem, one he needed to think about before determining how best to resolve it.

They entered his office just as Catherine's cell phone rang. "Excuse me a minute," she murmured. After answering the call, she listened at length, her expression growing more and more concerned. "Thanks. I'll take it from here."

"Problem?" he asked once she'd disconnected the call.

"I have the Collington wedding scheduled for a week from tomorrow. The bride just called in to cancel our services."

"At this late date?"

Catherine shook her head. "Obviously, she heard about what happened at the Marconis' and it's panicked her. Di—my partner managed to get her to agree to meet with me for lunch."

"I'll go with you."

To his surprise, she didn't argue. "Normally, I'd be able to handle it. Brides are often in crazy mode by now. I'm used to it."

"But trying to calm her down after hearing about everything that went wrong with Natalie's party…"

"Will prove challenging. Fortunately, I have an ace in the hole." She smiled, the first natural one she'd offered since their argument. "You. You've always had a way about you, an ability to smooth ruffled feathers."

"I'll do my best." He checked his watch. "Your partner is late."

"Maybe she hit traffic."

"You're sure she's coming?"

"She was in the city when she called me just now."

Right on cue, voices reverberated through the thick wooden door panels, one irritated, clearly Roxanne. Gabe winced. His assistant wasn't at her best this morning. The other, a voice he'd known for every one of this thirty-three years, snapped back with impatient authority. His office door banged open, and his mother paused with her hand on the knob.

"I know the way into my own son's office, Roxy," she informed Gabe's assistant.

"It's Roxanne."

"Well, maybe when you've worked here awhile I'll remember your name."

Gabe could see his assistant visibly struggling to hang on to her composure. She managed it. Barely. "He has a meeting scheduled, Mrs. Piretti. And just to set the record straight, I've worked here for three years, as I'm certain you're well aware."

"Huh. Could have sworn you were one of those annoying temps." With that Dina slammed the door in Roxanne's face. Turning, she offered a broad, delighted smile. "Gabriel, Catherine. It's so good to see the two of you together again. Give me a minute to just stand here and enjoy the view."

Gabe's lips twitched. "I'm sorry, Mom, but Roxanne was right. We're waiting for Catherine's business partner to join us in order to—" He broke off as the connection clicked into place, a connection he would have made long ago if he hadn't been so distracted by the apprehensive woman standing at his side. "No. Oh, *hell,* no. You're not... You can't be—"

Dina stuck out her hand. "Dina Piretti, co-owner of Elegant Events. So good of you to help us with our small financial crisis."

* * *

The meeting didn't last long. The minute Dina exited the room, Gabe turned on Catherine. "My *mother?* You dumped me, and then you went into business with my *mother?*"

Catherine struggled not to flinch. "Really, Gabe. I don't see what one thing has to do with the other."

"You don't see—" He forked his fingers through his hair, turning order into all-too-attractive, not to mention distracting, disorder. "You must have suspected I wouldn't like the idea considering that the two of you have been careful to keep me in the dark for nearly two years now. Why is that, Cate?"

She planted her hands on her hips. "You want logic? Fine. Here's some logic for you. I didn't want to see you. If you knew I was in business with your mother, you wouldn't have been able to stay away. Worse, you might have tried to interfere, or…I don't know—" She waved a hand through the air. "Tried to protect her from me and stopped us from doing business together."

"You're damn right I would have stopped you from doing business together," he retorted. "But not for the reason you think. It isn't my mother I would have wanted to protect. It's you."

That stopped her cold. "What are you talking about?"

"I told you that I had to step in and take over Piretti's," he began.

"Right." He'd never gone into details, other than to inform her that it had been one of the toughest periods in his life. But she'd been able to read between the lines. "After your father died."

He shook his head. "Not exactly. After he died, my mother took over."

That caught her by surprise, not that it caused her any real concern. "So? She's brilliant."

"Yes, she is. What I never told you before was that she brilliantly ran Piretti's to the verge of bankruptcy. That's when I seized control."

Uh-oh. That didn't sound good. "Seized. You mean—" She struggled to come up with a more palatable word. "Took charge."

His mouth tightened. "No, I mean I swooped in and instigated a hostile takeover. You've teased me often enough about my nickname, but you never came right out and asked where I got it." He lowered his head and rubbed a hand along the nape of his neck. "Well, that's where."

She approached and rested a hand on his arm. She could feel the muscles bunching beneath her fingers, his tension palpable. "I can't believe you'd have done such a thing unless it was absolutely necessary. What happened, Gabe? Why were you forced to such extremes?"

He stilled. "Catherine." Just her name, spoken so softly, with such a wealth of emotion behind it. He lifted his head and looked at her. The intensity of his gaze mesmerized her, the shade of blue so brilliant it put the sky to shame. "You show such faith. Not a single doubt. Not a single hesitation. How can you think what's between us is temporary?"

"I know you." The admission slipped out on a whisper. "I know what sort of man you are."

"I'm hard and ruthless."

"True."

"I take apart companies."

"And put them back together again."

The smallest hint of a smile played about his mouth, easing some of the tension. "Or make them a part of Piretti's."

"Well, you are a businessman, first and foremost." Sorrow filled her. "And that's why I say our relationship is temporary. Because Piretti's isn't just a place where you work. It's who and what you are."

The tension stormed back. "There hasn't been any other choice. I had to take the business away from her."

She drew him over to the couch and sat down with him. "Explain it to me," she encouraged.

"You are right about one thing. My mother is a brilliant business woman. When it comes to numbers and accounting and contracts, there's no one better."

"But…?"

"But she's too damn nice."

"Yeah, I hate that about her, too," Catherine teased.

The grin was back, one identical to his mother's. "That soft heart means people can take advantage of her."

"And they did."

He nodded. "After my father died she began staffing Piretti's with friends and family. Nepotism became the byword."

Catherine tried to put herself in Dina's shoes. "It

probably comforted her to have loved ones around at such a time."

He started to say something, paused, then frowned. "Huh. I never considered that possibility, but looking back, you may be right."

"I am right. Dina told me so one evening." Catherine interlaced her fingers with his, needing to touch him. She suspected he needed the physical contact as well. "I think it was on the fifth anniversary of your dad's death. She was having a rough night, and we talked about all sorts of things. It was one of the few times she mentioned Piretti's."

"Taking the business away from her nearly killed her." Pain bled through the words. "I did that to her. I did that to my own mother."

Catherine frowned in concern. "Were her friends and family members incompetent?"

"Not all. Those who were took gross advantage. She paid them ludicrous salaries for jobs they, at best, neglected, and at worst didn't perform at all. They'd put in a few hours and then take off. That forced Mom to hire more people to do the jobs that weren't getting done."

"Which explains why you refuse to mix business and pleasure." It explained so much. "Couldn't you have simply come in and cleaned house?"

"If she'd let me, yes. But there was the board of directors to consider."

Understanding dawned. "Let me guess. The board comprised those individuals who were taking advantage of her. And they weren't about to let you mess with the status quo."

"Got it in one."

Compassion filled her. "So the only solution was for Gabe 'the Pirate' Piretti to raid the company."

"I cleaned house, all right. Starting right at the top with my mother and working down from there."

"How did Dina handle it when you took over?"

"She was furious. She wouldn't even speak to me. So, I abducted her."

Catherine's eyes widened. "Excuse me? You what?"

"I loaded her into my car, protesting all the way, and took her off to a resort and forced her to deal with the situation. Of course, the daily massages and mai tais— heavy on the rum—didn't hurt. It also helped that I brought along the accounts and forced her to look at the bottom line." He shot her a cool look. "I've considered using the same approach with you in order to get to the bottom of some of our issues."

She released his hand and swept to her feet. "It wouldn't have worked."

His eyes narrowed. "And there's that secret again, right smack-dab between us." He rose as well. "How many mai tais would it take to pry it out of you, Catherine?"

She shook her head. "There's nothing to pry out. I told you. Your view of marriage and what you want from it are a hundred and eighty degrees different from my wants and needs."

"You know one of the qualities that makes me such a good pirate?" He didn't wait for her to respond. "I'm excellent at reading people."

She took a step backward. "Not all people."

"You'd be surprised." He followed in the path of her retreat. "For instance, it only takes one look for me to know that you're lying. You're keeping something from me, and all the denials in the world aren't going to convince me otherwise."

"Too bad. You'll just have to live with it."

"For instance…" He trapped her against one of the huge picture windows overlooking the sound. Brilliant light encased them, sparkling over and around them. "I know for a fact that you've always wanted children. You told me so yourself."

She forced her gaze to remain steady, to be captured and held by his. "Long ago. In another lifetime. But I've changed since then. My wants and needs have changed, as well." She forced out a laugh. "I find it ridiculous to have to explain this to you, of all people. You, who puts business ahead of everything and everyone. Why is it acceptable for you and not for me?"

"Because it's not true."

He leaned in. Even with layers of clothing separating them, she could feel the heat of his body, feel the sinful contours that were so potently male. And then he made it so much worse. He slid his hand low on her abdomen, his fingers spread wide across the flat surface. She shuddered beneath his touch, her belly quivering in response. Liquid heat pooled, stealing thought and reason.

"Are you telling me you don't want any children at all? Not even one?"

She forced out the lie. "No, not even one."

A lazy smile crept across his mouth, one that told her

he didn't believe a word of it. He dropped his head, his mouth brushing along the sensitive skin of her throat, just beneath her ear where her pulse skipped and raced. "You don't ever want to give birth?" The question burned like acid. "You don't want to feel your womb swell with our baby? Feel the flutter of new life? Sing and talk to him while he grows and becomes? Encourage his passage from his safe little nest into a world just waiting for his arrival?"

Dear God, make him stop, she silently prayed. She fixed her eyes on a point just over his shoulder and took a long, calming breath. "That's what you want, isn't it?"

"More than you can possibly imagine."

One more slow breath and she'd worked up the courage to shift her eyes to his. It took everything she possessed not to respond to the rich warmth of those impossibly blue eyes. "Then I suggest you start looking for someone who can give that to you. Because it's not going to be me." She spread her hands across his chest and nudged him back a few inches. "Look at me, Gabe. Look at me and tell me I'm lying to you. I won't give you a child. Not ever. Is that clear enough for you?"

His hand slid from her abdomen and he stepped back. "Quite clear." His face fell into hard, taut lines. "And quite honest."

"Thank you for recognizing it." She twitched her blouse into place and smoothed her skirt. "And thank you for admitting as much."

The phone on his desk gave a soft purring ring. He

crossed to answer it. Listening a moment, Gabe said, "Put him through." Then he covered the receiver. "I'm sorry, but I have to take this call."

She slipped behind her most professional demeanor. "Of course. I'll wait for you in the foyer."

He stopped her just as she reached for the doorknob. "Catherine? If you think our discussion has changed my mind about our relationship, you're wrong."

She glanced over her shoulder. "Why? Because you think at some point in the future I'm going to change my mind?" She could see from his expression that was precisely what he thought. A smile escaped, one of infinite regret. "Let me clue you in and save both of us a lot of time and grief. I won't."

And with that, she escaped his office.

Closing the door behind her, Catherine took a quick breath. As long as her day was progressing so well, she might as well keep the streak going. The time had come to deal with Roxanne. Either they came to terms here and now or Catherine would take action. But never again would she step back and take it on the chin. Never again would she allow this woman to cause harm to her business or make her life the misery it had been during those earlier years.

She paused by Roxanne's desk, fully aware that she'd been noticed and equally as aware that she wouldn't be acknowledged any time soon. It was unquestionably a power play, one Catherine intended to commandeer.

"Hiding behind that computer screen isn't going to

make me go away. All it does is confirm that you're afraid to look me in the eye." It was the perfect gambit, Catherine thought with some satisfaction, causing Roxanne's head to jerk up and anger to flare to life in her sloe eyes. "You and I are going to get something straightened out."

"You're the one who needs to be straightened out. I—"

"I'm not interested in what you have to say," Catherine cut her off smoothly. "It's your turn to listen. Or shall we have this conversation in Gabe's office?"

"And talk about what?" she demanded. "Your whiny complaints about his favorite assistant? He's too logical to give them any credence."

"It's because he's so logical that he will." She gestured toward Gabe's closed door. "Shall we find out which of us is right?" She wasn't the least surprised when Roxanne didn't take her up on the offer.

"Where do you get off, threatening me?" she asked instead. "You have no idea who and what you're taking on."

Catherine planted her palms on Roxanne's desk and leaned in. "I know precisely who I'm taking on, and, sweetie, I knew what you were from day one. Now you close your mouth and listen very carefully, because I'm only going to say this once. If you mess with me or my business ever again, I will see to it that your career as you currently know it ends. I will make it my mission to introduce you to hell on earth."

"You don't have that power," Roxanne scoffed.

"Watch me."

Gabe's assistant leaned back in her chair and folded her arms across her chest, a smug smile playing about her generous mouth. "Is this about your little disaster at the Marconi party?"

"No, this is about *your* little disaster at the Marconi party. Specifically, the boaters whose advent you were so eager for me to witness."

Roxanne's smile grew, slow and catlike. "You can't prove I had anything to do with that."

"Can't I?" Catherine straightened and thrust her hand into her purse. Retrieving her cell phone, she flipped it open. One press of a button snapped a digital picture of Roxanne. Another press had it winging its way to Catherine's e-mail account.

Roxanne straightened in her chair. "What the hell did you just do?"

"I've e-mailed myself your photo. When I get home, I intend to print it off and hand-deliver it to the King County Sheriff's Marine Unit. They have some very contrite boaters who are eager to point the finger at the person who invited them to the Marconis' party and encouraged them to make—how did they phrase it? Oh, right. A splashy entrance." Roxanne turned deathly pale, and Catherine smiled. "Nothing to say? How incredibly unlike you."

It was too much to hope the silence would last. Roxanne recovered within seconds. "So what if I extended an invitation? It's their word against mine how it was phrased."

"You be sure to explain that technicality to Natalie Marconi...right after you explain your side of things to

Gabe. I doubt either of them will be terribly sympathetic considering the damage done."

"They won't believe you." An edge of desperation underscored the statement.

"Oh, I think they will. And once Natalie finds out you were behind the boat incident, I don't think it'll take much of a nudge to convince her to ask around and see if any of her guests happened to notice a very striking guest in an attention-grabbing red dress hanging around the sprinkler controls. I guarantee someone will have noticed you. That's what happens when you work so hard to be the center of attention. Sometimes you get it when you'd rather not have it." Catherine gave that a moment to sink in. "This ends and ends now. You keep your claws off my business. More importantly, you keep your mouth—and every other body part—off my man. And you stop setting up business appointments that interfere with our life together."

Roxanne fought to recover a hint of her old cockiness. "Spoiled your first night together, did I?" She released a sigh of mock disappointment. "Such a shame."

"Gabe more than made up for it this morning." That wiped the smile off her face. "I'm giving you precisely one week to convince Natalie that someone else is at fault for the events of last night, someone other than Elegant Events. You have seven days to convince her that somebody other than me sabotaged that party."

Roxanne's eyes widened in panic. "Have you lost your mind? How do you expect me to do that?"

"I don't know, and I don't care. You've always been fast on your feet and quick to spin a story. Find a way."

"What if I refuse your…request?"

"It wasn't a request. In one week's time, I act. I start with the sheriff, and I end with a lawyer. And somewhere in between—one night in bed, perhaps—I'll wonder out loud whether you're the type of person Gabe wants representing Piretti's. Seeds like that have an uncanny knack of taking root."

"If I do what you want…" The words escaped like chewed glass. "What then?"

"Then you have two choices. Option number one, you can behave yourself and toe the line. For instance, I have an event coming up this next weekend, assuming Gabe and I can salvage the account. You are not going to interfere with that event in any way, shape or form. If anything goes wrong, just the least little thing, I'm putting it on you. I don't care if it decides to rain that day, it'll be your fault. If Mt. Rainier turns active and dumps ash all over Annie Collington's special day…your fault. If anything goes wrong, I promise, I will bury you for it."

One look at Roxanne's face told the story. She'd planned to do something. Catherine could only imagine what that might be. "You said I have two choices," she replied. "What's my other one?"

"You can pack up your brimstone and find a new boss to screw with."

"You can't fire me. Only Gabe can."

Catherine smiled in real pleasure. "Now, that's my favorite part about our little dilemma here, because you're right. I don't have that ability. So I thought of the perfect way around that small stumbling block. You see, men always have so much trouble deciding on the perfect wedding gift for their bride." Not that he'd asked. But Roxanne didn't have to know that. "Lucky for Gabe, now I know exactly what I want. And I guarantee he'll accommodate my request."

"You bitch!"

Catherine's amusement faded. "You're damn right. I'm through playing nice. And in case you still have any doubts, let me assure you that the benefits of bitchdom keep adding up." She gave it to her, chapter and verse. "If you try and start any more trouble after you leave Piretti's, people will immediately conclude that it's sour grapes on your part. And if they have the least little doubt, I'll be sure to explain it first to them, and then to my lawyer." She released her breath in a happy little sigh. "See how simple all this is?"

"This isn't over, you—" She broke off and to Catherine's shock, huge tears filled her eyes. "Oh, Gabe. I'm so sorry you have to see us like this."

He stood in the doorway, his gaze shifting from one woman to the other. "Problem?"

"Not yet," Catherine said.

She kept Roxanne pinned with a hard look. She held up her phone as a pointed reminder and then made a production of returning it to her purse. It was a subtle warning, but it seemed to have a profound effect. Satisfied that they understood each other, Catherine turned and offered Gabe a sunny smile.

"No problem at all," she assured him. "Roxanne and I were simply coming to a long-overdue understanding."

He folded his arms across his chest. "That explains the tears."

"Exactly," she stated serenely. "Tears of joy. We're both all choked up with emotion."

"Uh-huh. So I see." She wished she could read his expression, but he'd assumed the indecipherable mask he wore during his most intense business negotiations. "Roxanne? Anything to add?"

His assistant ground her teeth in frustration, but managed a hard, cold smile. "Not a thing. At least, not yet."

"Excellent." He inclined his head toward the elevators. "Ready, Catherine?"

"As ready as I'll ever be."

"Then off we go before you cause any more tears of joy."

Seven

Catherine gave Gabe directions to the little café just north of the city, where arrangements had been made to meet with the bride-to-be. Annie Collington, a bubbly redhead with a smattering of freckles across the bridge of her upturned nose, appeared tense and unhappy.

Introductions were made, and Annie smiled at Gabe with only a hint of her customary zest. "I recognize you, of course. I think your photo is on everything from the society page to the business section to the gossip magazines."

"I wouldn't believe a word of anything except the gossip magazines."

She twinkled briefly before she caught Catherine's eye and her amusement faded. "Do we really have to do this?" she asked miserably. "I've fired you, now that's the end of it. Nothing you say is going to change my mind."

Before Catherine could respond, Gabe stepped in smoothly. "Why don't we sit down and have a cup of coffee and a bite to eat while we figure out how best to settle this?"

"Please, Annie." Catherine added gentle pressure. "Your wedding is only eight days away. You have such a beautiful day planned. You don't want to make any rash decisions that might jeopardize it."

"That's precisely what I'm trying to prevent," Annie insisted. "I heard about the Marconi party. It was a disaster. I can't have that happen at my wedding."

"And it won't," Gabe assured her. Without even seeming to do so, he guided them to the table the hostess had waiting for them, seated them, and ordered coffee and a platter of house specialty sandwiches. "May I make a proposal that might help with your decision?" he asked Annie.

"Gabe—" Catherine began.

"No, it's okay," Annie interrupted. "He can try."

Catherine fell silent, struggling to suppress an irrational annoyance. After all, Gabe was just trying to help, even if it did feel as if he'd swooped in and taken command of her meeting. Still, she didn't appreciate him seizing control like…well, like a damn pirate.

"How about this, Annie?" Gabe was saying. "If you agree to continue to use Catherine and Elegant Events as your wedding planner, I will personally guarantee that your wedding goes off without a hitch."

"You can't do that," Catherine instantly protested.

"You can do that?" Annie asked at the same time.

"I can, absolutely."

The coffee arrived in a slender, wafer-thin porcelain urn hand-painted with an intricate pattern of wild red strawberries and crisp green leaves. After aiming a dazzling smile of dismissal in the direction of their waitress, Gabe took over the chore of pouring fragrant cups for the three of them. The delicate bits of china should have looked small and clumsy in his large hands. But instead he manipulated the coffee service with an impressive dexterity that made him appear all the more powerful and male. He made short work of the chore, and Catherine could see that she wasn't the only one dazzled by the way his raw masculinity dominated and subdued the fussy bit of femininity.

"Let's see if this offer doesn't appeal," he said as he handed Annie her cup. "If you're not one hundred per-cent satisfied with your wedding, I'll personally see to it that you're refunded every penny."

She accepted the coffee with a smile. "That doesn't exactly guarantee that it'll go off without a hitch," she pointed out with impressive logic.

"True," Gabe conceded, while Catherine silently steamed at his high-handedness.

She didn't want or need anyone to guarantee her ability to pull off this wedding. She was capable. Competent. She knew the business inside and out. But with one simple offer, he'd reduced Elegant Events in the eyes of her client to a struggling start-up in need of a "real" businessman to back its ability to perform successfully.

Gabe relaxed in his chair, very much in charge. "I may not be able to guarantee that nothing will go wrong if you honor your contract. But understand this, Annie. There is one thing I *can* guarantee." He paused to add weight to his comment. "Your wedding will be an unmitigated disaster if you try and do it on your own at this late stage. You're just asking for trouble attempting to be both bride and coordinator."

Annie gnawed on her bottom lip. Clearly, the same thought had occurred to her. "I might be able to pull it off," she offered.

"You think so? Then I suggest you consider this…"

He turned the full battery of Piretti charm and business savvy on her and Catherine watched in amused exasperation. Annie didn't stand a chance against him, poor thing. She hung on his words, her eyes huge as she tumbled under his spell like every other woman who'd come up against those devilish blue eyes and persuasive personality.

"After what happened at the Marconi party, Catherine is strongly motivated to make certain your wedding is perfect in every regard, if only to prove that her reputation for excellence remains intact."

Catherine shot Gabe a quelling glare. Not that it did much to quell him. The man was unquellable. "I can't go into specifics about what happened," she explained to Annie, deftly assuming control. "But I want to assure you that the problems we experienced were not a result of anything I did wrong, but for the most part caused by some mischief maker out to amuse him- or herself by turning on the sprinklers. On top of that there were a few boaters who crashed the party. I know this is a stressful time for you. And I don't doubt you're under tremendous pressure."

"My mother's insisting I get rid of you," Annie admitted. "And since she's the one paying…"

"If you'd like me to meet with her and address her concerns, I will."

Annie gave it a moment's thought before shaking her head. "No, that won't be necessary. One of the agreements Mom and I came to about the wedding was that it was my wedding. I get to make the decisions." Her gamine smile flashed. "She gets to pay for them."

Catherine responded with an answering smile and gave one more gentle push. "In that case, I hope you'll decide to honor our contract." She kept her eyes trained on Annie's, hoping the younger girl would see Catherine's sincerity, as well as her determination. "I promise to do my absolute best for you."

"But Gabe's guarantee stands, right?"

Catherine gritted her teeth. "Gabe's guarantee stands."

"In that case…" Annie beamed. "Okay."

"Then it's settled? We move forward?"

"It's settled. You can stay on as my event stager." Her attention switched to Gabe and she shot him an impish look. "Although I have to admit I'm almost hoping something does go wrong so you're stuck footing the bill."

He leaned in. "I'll see what I can do to sabotage

something," he said in a stage whisper. "Something that won't cause too much trouble, but just enough to get you off the hook."

Annie giggled. "Nah, don't do that. It would only make me feel guilty, afterward. If you can make sure there aren't any screwups, that's all that matters to me."

"Gabe won't have to worry about it," Catherine inserted smoothly. "That's my job." She leveled Gabe with a single look. "And it's a job I do quite well."

Lunch sped by, though afterward Catherine couldn't have said what they talked about or even what they ate. While part of her was grateful for Gabe's assistance—after all, he'd rescued the account, hadn't he? The other part, the major part, was hands-down furious.

"Go on," he said the minute they parted company with Annie and were walking toward his Jag. "What's eating you?"

She didn't bother to hold back. "I realize you're accustomed to being in charge, but I'd appreciate it if you'd remember that this is *my* business."

He paused beside the passenger door, key in hand. "You resent my offering to guarantee a successful event?" he asked in surprise.

"To be blunt, yes. I felt like a teenager purchasing her first car and needing Daddy to cosign the loan agreement."

He considered that for a minute. "Perhaps it would help if you examined it from a slightly different angle."

She folded her arms across her chest. What other angle was there? "What other angle is there?"

"I'm a businessman. It goes against the grain to lose

money." He thought about it, and added, "It more than goes against the grain."

"Then you better hope everything proceeds without a hitch, because otherwise you'll be on the hook for…" She silently performed a few mathematical gymnastics and named a total that left him blanching. "Weddings don't come cheap," she informed him. "Especially not ones I stage."

"Why don't they just buy a house?" he argued. "It would last longer and one day show a return on investment."

"Fortunately for Elegant Events that doesn't occur to most couples."

He brushed that aside. "My point is…my offer to guarantee your success shows the extent of my confidence in you and Elegant Events. I don't back losers, and I don't have any intention of paying for Annie's wedding. Nor will I have to because I know you. I know you'll do an outstanding job."

Catherine opened her mouth to reply and then shut it again. "Huh."

He closed the distance between them, trapping her against the car. "I have faith in you, sweetheart. There's not a doubt in my mind that Saturday's wedding is going to be a dream come true for our young Annie. And I think it's all going to be thanks to you."

"You really believe that?" she asked, touched.

The intensity of his gaze increased. "I've always believed in you, and one of these days you're going to let me prove that to you."

She barely had time to absorb that before he lowered his head and caught her mouth in a kiss so tender it brought tears to her eyes. He believed in her, had done his best to demonstrate that today. And what had she given him in return? Doubt. Mistrust. Secrets. As much as she feared attempting that first, wobbly step to reestablish their relationship, maybe it was time to take a small leap of faith. Gabe was reaching out. Maybe, just maybe, she could do the same.

And with that thought it mind, she surrendered to the embrace and opened herself to possibilities. Opened herself to the dream.

The next week flew by. To Gabe's amusement, he realized that Catherine was doing just as he'd predicted. She threw every ounce of energy, focus and determination into making Annie's wedding as perfect as possible. She double- and triple-checked every detail. Then she checked again. She ran through endless scenarios of potential problems that could crop up, endless possibilities that might occur at the last instant. She knew she'd be under intense scrutiny, that any tiny flaw would be blown up into a major catastrophe. Annie's mother, in particular, was already proving a handful with endless phone calls and demands. And yet Gabe noticed that Catherine dealt calmly with every problem and complaint, not allowing her demeanor to be anything other than polite and reassuring.

"You're driving yourself to exhaustion," he told her toward the end of the week. He sank his fingers into the rigid muscles of her shoulders and worked to smooth out the knots and kinks. "You don't want that exhaustion to show, and the best way of avoiding that is to get some sleep."

Catherine nodded absently. "You're right. I'll join you in a minute. I just want to go over the seating chart one final time."

Without a word, he lifted her into his arms and carried her—protesting all the way—into the bedroom. "The seating chart will still be there in the morning, as will the menu and the flower order and the final head count. There's nothing more you can do tonight other than fuss."

"I do not fuss," she argued. "I organize."

"Sweetheart, I know organizing. That wasn't it. That was fussing."

She sagged against him. "You're right, you're right. I'm fussing. I can't seem to stop myself."

"That's what I'm here for."

He lowered Catherine onto the bed and in less than thirty seconds had her stripped and a wisp of a nightgown tugged over her slender form. Then he tucked her under the covers. He joined her ten seconds later, but by that time she'd already fallen sound asleep. Thank God for small miracles, he couldn't help but think. Sweeping her close, he brushed her hair back from her brow and planted a gentle kiss there. Satisfied that he'd accomplished his goal with minimal effort, he cushioned her head against his shoulder and allowed sleep to consume him as well.

As the end of the week approached, Gabe kept a

weather eye on Catherine, ensuring that she ate properly and caught as much sleep as possible. She tolerated his interference, seemed amused by it, even. Perhaps she understood that it originated from concern. And that gave him hope that maybe this time around they'd get their relationship right.

By Friday morning, the day of the reception, Catherine's calm had vanished and her nerves had shredded through her self-control. "Anything I can do?" he asked over breakfast.

She shook her head. "I have some paperwork to take care of this morning—"

"You and I both know it's all in order."

She flashed a brief, tense smile. "True. But I'm going to review it, anyway. Late this morning I'll head over to Milano's and finalize the arrangements for tomorrow's reception. Joe's outstanding at his job, so I don't doubt everything will be perfect, but—"

"You'll feel better after making sure." Gabe nodded in complete understanding. "What about tonight's rehearsal dinner?"

"That's the responsibility of the groom's family, thank goodness. Once the rehearsal is out of the way, I'll come home." He could see her do a mental run-through of her to-do list and wondered if she even noticed that she'd fallen into the habit of calling the apartment "home." "I want to try for an early night, which shouldn't be a problem. There will be a few last-minute phone calls to make before turning in, just to confirm everyone knows what time they need to show up tomorrow."

He covered her hand with his. "No one will dare be late."

She relaxed enough to offer a genuine smile. "You're right about that. It's not wise to tick off a woman clinging to the edge of a cliff by a fingernail."

His grin faded, replaced by concern. "That bad?"

She hesitated, then shook her head. "Not really," she confessed. "I've got two or three fingernails firmly dug in."

Maybe he could help with that. "I want to escort you to the wedding tomorrow, Cate."

She stared blankly. "I'll be working."

"I understand. But I'd like to be there to offer moral support, as well as give you another set of hands should there be a snag."

A frown formed between her eyebrows. "People will think I can't handle my own business," she argued.

"I'll keep a low profile."

"Right," she said in exasperation. "Because, goodness knows, no one in Seattle will recognize Gabe 'the Pirate' Piretti."

He tried another tack. "My presence might help keep Annie's mother in check."

"I can handle Beth," Catherine grumbled.

"I don't doubt it. But it might force her to think twice before causing trouble or throwing a fit over some trifling problem."

Catherine turned white. "There will be *no* trifling problems. There will be *no* problems at all."

Hell. "That's what I meant to say," he hastened to reassure her. "I'll just be your muscle."

To his relief, she relaxed ever so slightly, and her smile flashed again. "Fine. You can be my muscle. Muscle remains in the background and blends in with the wallpaper."

"Got it. I can do wallpaper."

Catherine simply shook her head in open amusement. "Good try, but you couldn't do wallpaper if your life depended on it."

He lifted her hand and kissed it. "Why, thank you, darling. Allow me to return the compliment."

She visibly softened. "You don't have to come, Gabe. I won't need help."

"You're right, you won't. But I want to be there for you."

She debated for a few seconds before nodding. "Fine. This one time you can come."

He struggled to appear both humble and grateful. If she hadn't been so distracted, she wouldn't have bought it for a minute. "I appreciate it." That decided, he pushed back from the table. Bending down, he tipped her chin upward and gave her a slow, thorough kiss. "I'm off to work. If you need me, call my cell."

She stopped him before he'd gone more than a half dozen steps. "Gabe?" When he turned, she smiled in a way that had his gut clenching.

"Thanks."

The day of Annie's wedding proved perfect in every regard. The weather couldn't have been prettier. Everyone showed up exactly on time. And best of all, the entire affair ran like clockwork. To Catherine's relief, her nerves settled the minute she stepped foot in the church. She fell into a comfortable rhythm, orchestrating the progression with an ease and skill that impressed even Annie's mother.

There were the expected last-minute glitches. Someone stashed the bridal bouquet in the wrong room, causing momentary panic. The ring bearer managed to get grass stains on his britches during the ten seconds his mother wasn't supervising him. And one of the bridesmaids caught her heel in the hem of her gown and needed last-minute stitching. But other than that, the flow continued toward its inevitable conclusion, slow and smooth and golden.

Once the ceremony began, she had a moment to catch her breath and stood in the vestibule with Gabe, watching the timeless tradition of sacred words and new beginnings. It never failed to move her, and this time was no different.

"We never quite got there, did we?" Gabe said in an undertone.

It had been a long day. An exhausting week. Perhaps because of it, the question struck with devastating accuracy. "No," she whispered. "We never did."

The couple had reached the point where they were exchanging their vows, promises to love and cherish through good times and bad. When she and Gabe had hit those rough patches, she hadn't stuck. She'd run.

"We're not going to ever get there," he informed her in a quiet voice. "Not the way we're going. In order for a couple to marry, they have to trust each other. And we don't."

She fought to keep the tremble from her voice. "I know."

He leaned in, his presence a tangible force. "We have a choice, sweetheart. We can walk away now. No harm, no foul." He let that sink in before continuing. "Or we can do what we should have done two years ago. We can fight for it."

Would he still feel the same way if he had all the facts at his disposal? She doubted it. And now wasn't the time to find out. "I don't trust easily," she admitted. "Not anymore. I've spent two years building up walls."

"There are ways around walls. Chinks and cracks we can squeeze through. If it doesn't work out between us, you can always seal up all those cracks again."

"True."

"Are you willing to try, Cate?" His hands dropped to her shoulders and he turned her to face him. "Will you give it an honest try?"

She wanted to. Oh, how she longed to do just that. "I'd like to. But there are things—"

His mouth tightened for a telling moment. "I'm well aware there are 'things.' I'm not asking you to explain until you're ready."

A wistful smile quivered on her lips and she shook her head in a combination of affection and exasperation. "I know you, Gabe. What you really mean is I can explain when I'm ready, so long as I'm ready on demand. Am I close?"

He conceded the observation with a shrug. "We can't resolve our differences until I know what the problem is."

He had a point.

"Will you give me a little more time?" Time to see whether their relationship had a shot at working before she unburdened herself. "I need to be convinced we can straighten out our previous problems before introducing new ones. I need to be certain it's real."

"It is real. But if time is what you need, I'll give it to you. For now." He held out his hand. "Shall we make it official?"

"You have a deal, Mr. Piretti."

She took the hand he offered, not the least surprised when he gave it a little tug. She allowed herself to sink against him. Then she lifted her face to his and sealed the agreement in a long, lingering kiss, a kiss that spoke to her on endless levels. The gentleness of it made a promise, one that she longed to believe, while the strength and confidence had her relaxing into the embrace. It contained an unspoken assurance that she could lean on him and he'd be there to gather her up. That she could tell him anything and everything and he'd understand. But there was another quality underlying the kiss, the strongest quality of all. Passion. It ribboned through the heated melding of lips, barely leashed.

"Cate…" Her name escaped in a harsh whisper, one filled with need. "How can you deny this? How can you doubt?"

"I don't deny it." It would be ridiculous to try, not when he could feel her helpless reaction to his touch. "But—"

"No, Catherine. No more excuses." He cupped her

face and fixed her with a determined gaze. "Make a choice. Right here, right now. Give us a chance."

She'd spent two long, lonely years getting over Gabe. Out of sheer protection, she'd shut that door and locked it, and she'd been determined to never open it again. Now here she was, forced to deal with all that she'd put behind her. Gabe didn't just want her to open that door to the past, he wanted to storm through.

She shivered. What would happen when he uncovered the secrets she kept hidden there? Would it make a difference? Or would a miracle happen? Was it possible for them to come to terms with the past? To readjust their priorities and choose each other over their careers? Or would they slowly, relentlessly slip back into old patterns?

There was only one way to find out. With the softest of sighs, Catherine closed her eyes and surrendered to the dream. "All right. I'll give us a chance."

Eight

It had become almost a ritual, Catherine decided. The long elevator ride to the executive floor of Piretti's office building, the brisk sweep across plush carpeting toward Roxanne's desk, the brief feminine clash of gazes and then the welcome that waited for her on the other side of Gabe's door.

Unlike the previous week, this time Roxanne stopped her, putting an unwelcome kink in the ritual. "Did she call you?" Her usual honeyed accent was missing, replaced by a tone both tight and abrupt.

Catherine paused. "If you mean Natalie, yes, she did."

Coal-black eyes burned with resentment. "That ends it, then?"

"That's entirely up to you."

She didn't wait for a reply but gave Gabe's door a light tap and walked in. He stood in his usual position at the windows, talking on his headset, and she could tell he hadn't heard her knock. She didn't think she'd ever tire of seeing him like this, a man in his element, captain of all he surveyed.

A hint of melancholy swept over her. He deserved so much more than she could give him. It was wrong of her to take advantage of him. Wrong of her to allow him to believe, even for this brief span of time, that they could forge a future together.

Even knowing all that, she couldn't seem to help herself. He'd asked her to try, and she intended to do precisely that, all the while knowing that she'd never have to reveal her secret because their relationship would never get that far. They'd hit a stumbling block long before it was time for true confessions.

The muscles across his back flexed the instant he became aware of her, and his head tilted as though he were scenting the air. He turned his head, his focus arrowing in her direction, and he smiled. Just that. Just a simple smile. And she melted.

What was it about him? Why Gabe and only Gabe? His personality was a big part of it, that forceful, take-charge persona that never saw obstacles, only challenges. But it wasn't only that. His intelligence attracted her, those brilliant leaps of insight and the instant comprehension of facts and figures, people and events. And then there was that raw sex appeal, his ability to ignite her with a single touch. She closed her eyes. Or a single look. Just being this close to him left her drunk with desire, the need for more a craving she'd never quite overcome.

"I'll get back to you tomorrow," he murmured into his headset, before disengaging. "What is it, Catherine? What's wrong?"

She forced herself to look at him and accept what couldn't be changed. "Nothing's wrong," she replied calmly. "In fact, something's very right."

He lifted an eyebrow and pulled off the headset, tossing it aside. "Good news? I'm all for that. What happened?"

"I had a call from Natalie Marconi this morning. It seems she's had a change of heart. She's discussed the situation with a number of her friends and decided that Elegant Events did a marvelous job, after all, and that the series of catastrophes that occurred were neither our fault, nor could we have prevented them."

Instead of appearing relieved, Gabe frowned. "That's a rather dramatic turnaround, considering her attitude the day after her party. Do you know what prompted it, other than a bit of time and conversation?"

Catherine prowled across his office to the well-stocked wet bar adjacent to the sitting area. Gabe got there ahead of her and poured her a glass of merlot. "Thanks." She took an appreciative sip. "From what I can gather, the suggestion has been made that someone deliberately caused the problems at her party in order to make Elegant Events appear incompetent."

"Interesting. And why, according to Natalie and her cronies, would someone do that?"

"Natalie is of the opinion that it's one of my competitors." Her comment caused surprise to bloom across his face and his frown to deepen. "Apparently, she'd been warned prior to the party not to hire me, but chose not to listen to the advice. She thinks the incidents were retribution."

He puzzled through that, his head bent, his fists planted on his hips, before shaking his head. "I don't like this, Catherine. It doesn't feel right to me. Just off the top of my head, I can think of a half dozen methods for undercutting someone in the business world that are far more effective than ruining a client's party. There are way too many risks setting up the sort of problems you experienced. Too many chances of getting caught. Too many potential witnesses who could point the finger in your direction. It's sloppy and nowhere near as effective as, say, undercutting your prices." He shook his head again. "No. This sort of reprisal, assuming it is a reprisal and not a series of unfortunate accidents, feels personal, not business related."

Unfortunately, he was right. It was personal. One more thing bothered her and bothered her a lot. She didn't care for Roxanne blaming other event planners. They were innocent in all this, and if the gossip adversely impacted their business, she'd have to find a way to set the record straight. Worse, she'd have to assume a small portion of the blame, since she'd ordered Roxanne to correct the problem, without putting any conditions on how she went about it.

Gabe seemed to reach a decision. "Let it go for now, Catherine. If Natalie is willing to forgive and forget, and better yet, give you a glowing recommendation, it can only help."

She stilled, eyeing him with open suspicion. "I know you, Gabe, and I know that expression. You're planning something. What is it?"

"Not planning," he denied. "But I do intend to poke around a bit. Kick over a few rocks and see if anything slithers out. If Natalie is right and someone is trying to destroy your business, I want to know about it. And if it's personal, I damn well intend to get to the bottom of it." A grimness settled over him and had her stiffening. Anyone who saw his expression at that moment wouldn't question how or why he'd acquired his nickname. "And if I find out it's deliberate, there will be hell to pay."

Catherine considered that for a moment and decided it worked for her. She hadn't asked for his help. She hadn't so much as hinted in that direction. Nor had she anticipated him offering it. If Gabe chose to do some kicking and came across a certain snake wearing a smirk and a tight red dress, it wouldn't hurt her feelings, nor would she feel terribly guilty about the resulting fallout.

"Fine. Let's forget about all this for now and move on." She checked her watch and nodded in satisfaction. Five on the dot. She set aside her wineglass. "Time to go," she announced, crossing to his side.

She'd caught Gabe off guard and suppressed a smile at his confusion.

"Go?"

"Absolutely. Time to clock out or whatever it is you

do when you power down the mighty Piretti conglomerate. We have plans."

"Hell, I didn't realize. Sorry about that."

He reached for his PDA and she took it from his hand and tossed it aside. "You won't find the appointment in there."

That captured his attention. "What are you up to?" he asked, intrigued.

"It's a surprise. Are you interested?" She started toward the door, throwing an enticing smile over her shoulder. "Or would you rather work?"

He beat her to the door. Opening it, he ushered her through and didn't even glance Roxanne's way. "Close down shop" was all he said as they headed for the elevators.

It proved to be a magical evening. They strolled along the Seattle waterfront, taking in the sights with all the excitement and pleasure of a pair of tourists. There'd been a number of changes since they'd last taken the opportunity to visit. New, intriguing shops, refurbished restaurants, a small plaza that hadn't been there before.

Catherine couldn't recall afterward what they talked about. Nothing life-altering. Just the sweet, romantic exchanges a man and a woman share while establishing a relationship. The swift, intimate touches. The eye contact that said so much more than mere words. The flavor of the air, combined with the texture of the season, mingling with the unique scent of the man at her side. She knew it was a bonding ritual, and that she had no business bonding with Gabe. But she couldn't seem to help herself.

Eventually, they arrived at Milano's on the Sound, Joe's newest restaurant. He'd asked her to drop by some evening and see if it wouldn't be an acceptable venue for one of her future events. They entered the restaurant, a trendy building at the far end of one of Seattle's many piers, and Gabe lifted an eyebrow.

"Is this business or pleasure?" he asked in a neutral voice.

"Not really business," she assured him. "I'll come back another time to check it out more thoroughly, but not tonight." She caught his hand in hers. "Tonight's for us."

One of the aspects that she loved about Joe's restaurants was that he designed them with lovers in mind. She had never quite figured out how he pulled it off, but through the clever use of spacing, angles and elegant furnishings, he managed to create little clandestine nooks that gave the diner the impression of utter privacy.

The maître d' remembered her from the many events she'd scheduled at Milano's downtown restaurant, and clearly recognized Gabe. He greeted them both by name and, with a minimum of fuss, escorted them to an exclusive section reserved for VIPs. A deep-cushioned V-shaped bench faced windows overlooking Puget Sound and allowed them to sit side by side. And yet, because it was angled, they were still able to face each other.

"I'm curious," she said, once they were seated. "Would you have been angry if I'd chosen to eat here in order to check out the restaurant, as well as have a romantic dinner with you?"

"Not if you'd told me that was your intention." He accepted the wine list from the sommelier and after a moment's discussion, placed their order. Out on the Sound, a ferry plied the white capped chop, heading toward Bainbridge Island while the Olympics rose majestically against the horizon. "I think one of the problems I'm having is deciding how, when and where to separate business from pleasure."

She conceded his point with a wry grin. "Don't feel bad. So am I."

He regarded her in all seriousness. "How am I supposed to handle it, Catherine? I'd like to tell you about my day. It's a big part of who I am and what I enjoy doing. I want to share that aspect of myself with you. And I'd like to tell you about the progress I've made on your accounting records." He watched the ferry as it headed out, and the bustle of a tug returning to port, before switching his attention to her. "But I'm hesitant in case I cross that line, especially since I haven't quite figured out where you've drawn it."

"I haven't," she insisted, turning to face him more fully. "I think that's something we should discuss."

"Fine. Are you willing to discuss it here and now?"

Good question. She'd planned this as a romantic evening rather than a business meeting. But with two high-powered careers, finding a balance was paramount. "Let's discuss work over wine and then see if we can't move on from there."

He gave a brisk nod. "Agreed."

She almost laughed at the mannerism. It was so Gabe

Piretti, master negotiator. "Okay, here goes. Have you had a chance to look at my accounts?"

"I have."

He seemed troubled, so she gave him a gentle bump. "Did you find something wrong? Dina is always so meticulous, I can't believe she made a mistake."

"No, everything looks in order. It's just…" He hesitated. "You remember I told you that Natalie's deduction about a competitor being responsible for your problems felt wrong?" At her nod, he continued. "Your books appear in order. But they feel wrong to me. Off, somehow."

"Have you spoken to your mother about it?"

He shook his head. "Not yet. I need time to go through them a little more thoroughly first. I've been a bit distracted because of this upcoming buyout, so I haven't been able to give it my full attention." The wine arrived, was poured and tested, then accepted. "When's your next event? I want to make sure I schedule it in my PDA."

She played with the stem of her glass. "Two days. It's a small one. Under normal circumstances I wouldn't have taken the contract, but with all the problems I've been having, I didn't dare turn them down."

"Smart."

"After that there's a charity function later in the week. And Dina tells me that some of the people who called after the Marconi party wanting to cancel have changed their minds. It's clear that word is getting out, though I suspect some of the turnaround is thanks to your mother's way with people." She shifted closer to Gabe. "You're like that, too."

He draped his arm around her, and she rested her head on his shoulder. "Dad wasn't. He tended to be gruffer. No nonsense."

She toyed with her wineglass. "I've seen that side of you, too, particularly when it comes to business."

"It runs down the Piretti line." A slow smile built across his face and a distant look crept into his gaze. "It'll be interesting to see which of our sons and daughters carry on that tradition. Or maybe they'll be more like you. More passionate. Determined to take on the world."

"Oh, Gabe," she whispered.

He stiffened. "Damn. Damn it to hell." He gave a quick shake of his head. "I'm sorry, Catherine. That wasn't deliberate, it just popped out. I wasn't thinking."

"Don't. Don't apologize." She eased from his hold. "Don't you see, Gabe? It's part of who you are. Part of what you come from. You're a Piretti. Your family has been in this part of the country since the first settler felled the first log. You told me yourself that Piretti's was originally a sawmill."

"Times change," he said with a hint of imperiousness. "Now Piretti's is what I say it is."

"Your empire was built on a foundation of those who came before you," she argued. "You may have changed the scope and context of your family's business, but it's still a family concern."

"It's *my* concern," he corrected. "Where it goes from this point forward is wherever I choose to steer it."

"And in another thirty years?" she pressed. "In another forty? Who steers it then, Gabe?"

"In another thirty or forty years I'll have an answer for you," he replied with impressive calm. "Or maybe I'll follow Jack LaRue's example and sell out. Retire and live large."

"I can't believe you could simply let it all go after working so hard to build it up."

"Watch me."

She didn't believe him. "I know you, Gabe. You still want children. That little slip tells me that much. And it doesn't take a genius to see what course of action you've set. You think you'll be able to change my mind."

"Cards on the table, Cate?"

She snatched up her wineglass. "Oh, please."

"I do want children. Either you'll change your mind about that, or you won't. But understand this…" He paused, his face falling into uncompromising lines. "If it comes down to a choice between you and children, I choose you. Is that course of action clear enough for you?"

He didn't give her time to say anything more. He took her wineglass from her hand and returned it to the table. And then he pulled her into his arms and kissed her. Kissed her in a way that had every other thought fleeing from her head. Kissed her with a thoroughness she couldn't mistake for anything but total, undiluted passion. Kissed her until her entire world was this man and this moment.

"No more excuses," he growled, when they came up for air. He bit at her lip and then soothed it with his tongue. "No more barriers. I may have forced you to move in with me, forced you into this devil's contract, but you accepted the terms and by God, you'll honor them. I won't have you walking away from me because of some trumped-up excuse."

She fought for breath. "It's not an excuse."

He swore. "Anything and everything you use to shove a wedge between us is an excuse, and I'm not having any more of it. Try me, Catherine. Keep trying me. Because I swear to you, I will wipe each and every obstacle out of existence before I'll ever let you go again. I made the mistake of letting you run last time. This time I will follow you to the ends of the earth. I will follow you to hell and back, if that's what it takes."

She buried her head against his shoulder. "You're wrong, Gabe. You just don't know it yet. Next time, you won't just let me go. You'll throw me out."

Gabe couldn't help but notice that the tenor of their relationship changed after that. There'd always been barriers between them, but now they were so high and clear that he found himself stumbling over them at every turn. Despite that, two things gave him hope.

For one, Catherine continued with their impromptu dates, constantly surprising him with tickets to a play or dinners out or a picnic in their bedroom. Some occasions were brief, barely an hour, slipped into a narrow window in their schedules. Others were longer, partial days where they'd escape from work and spend endless hours enjoying each other's company. It made him realize that they could change. They could work around two diverse and demanding schedules.

The other thing that gave him hope was the nights they shared. For some reason, when they slid into bed and then into each other, all their differences, all their conflicts, faded from existence. There they joined and melded. There they found a true meeting of mind and body and spirit.

Later that week, he surprised her by showing up at one of her events, a charity fund-raiser for pediatric cancer patients. He'd expected to find her in her usual position, quietly in the background directing and coordinating the smooth progress of the affair. Instead, he found her sprawled on the floor, reading to a crowd of children from a Mrs. Pennywinkle picture book.

Tendrils of her hair had escaped its orderly knot and a succession of curls danced around her forehead and cheeks and at the vulnerable nape of her neck. Her eyes as she read were golden warm and sweetened with a soft generosity. There weren't any barriers here. Here he found her at her most open and natural. He'd seen her like this other times, almost invariably around children, and he shook his head in amusement. How could she claim to never want a child of her own when he could almost taste her longing, and could see the sheer joy she experienced light up the room?

She must have sensed him on some level because her head jerked up, like a doe sensing danger. Her gaze shot unerringly to his and for a brief second she shared that same openness with him that she'd shared with the children. And then the barriers slammed into place. He stood for a long moment, staring at her. It just about

killed him that she felt the need to protect herself from
him, and a fierce determination filled him.

Somehow, someway, he'd break through those
defenses. He'd win back her trust, and this time he'd do
everything in his power to keep it. He approached,
keeping his demeanor open and casual. Leaning down,
he gave her a light, easy kiss, one that elicited giggles
from their audience.

Catherine handed the book over to one of her assis-
tants and excused herself. Not that the children let her
go without a fight. She was swamped with hugs before
they reluctantly allowed her to leave.

He helped her up, drawing her close long enough to
murmur in her ear, "Have I told you recently how beautiful you are?"

Vivid roses bloomed in her cheeks. "Don't exagger-
ate, Gabe."

He tilted his head to one side. "You don't believe me,
do you?" The idea intrigued him.

"I'm attractive. Interesting looking, perhaps." She
stepped back. "But I'm not beautiful."

"You are to me," he stated simply.

To his amusement she changed the subject. "I didn't
expect to see you here. You never mentioned that you
might attend."

"I've been on the board of this particular charity for
a number of years, but I wasn't sure I could get away."
He cut her off before she could ask the question
hovering on her lips. "And no, I had nothing to do with
hiring you. That's handled by a subcommittee. I did

discover, however, that you've waived your usual fee and donated your services."

She shrugged. "It's for a good cause."

"Thank you." He could see her slipping back into professional mode and didn't want to distract her. "I'll let you get on with your duties. One quick question. What's your calendar for tomorrow look like?"

"I thought I might need a day off after the fund-raiser, so I kept it clear."

That suited him perfectly. After a few days of allowing Catherine to take the lead with their romantic outings, Gabe was intent on trying his hand at it. "Keep it that way, if you would."

She brightened. "You want me to plan something? Or shall we wing it?"

"I'll take care of everything. You just show up."

He gave her another swift kiss and then left her to focus on her event, though periodically through the afternoon he caught her glancing his way with a speculative look. Since they'd started in with the dates, he'd discovered that she preferred to keep their outings moving, no doubt so they wouldn't have another incident like the one at Milano's.

Come tomorrow, he intended to change all that.

All Gabe told Catherine in advance was to wear a swimsuit underneath her shorts and cotton tee and prepare for a day in the sun. When he pulled into Sunset Marina the next morning, she turned to him, her eyes glowing with pleasure.

"We're going for a cruise?"

"I thought we'd take a ride through the Chittenden locks and onto Lake Washington. Or we can wander around the Sound, if you prefer."

"It's been ages since I've gone through the locks. Let's do that."

The day became magical. In those precious hours, Gabe didn't care about the secrets that divided them, or the past or the future. The now occupied his full attention. It turned into one of those rare Seattle days where the Olympics stood out in sharp relief to the west and the Cascades held up their end to the east, with Mt. Rainier dominating the skyline in between. But as far as he was concerned the best view was the pint-sized woman who lazed across his foredeck. A hot golden sun blazed overhead, causing Catherine to strip down to her swimsuit, while a warm summer breeze stirred her hair into delightful disarray.

Eventually, she joined him on the bridge, handing him a soft drink and curling up in the seat next to him. She examined her surroundings with unmistakable pleasure. "I gather this is one of the custom-designed yachts your company manufactures."

"One of the smaller ones, yes." He shot her a swift grin. "It's not a Piretti engine…at least, not yet. I'm hoping to pin Jack LaRue down soon. Then maybe I'll have time to dig into your bookkeeping records and give them the attention they deserve."

She shrugged. "I'll leave that to you. It's definitely not my area of expertise, although it sure is Dina's."

"Mom has a talent for it," he agreed.

"I guess that's why it surprised me that she didn't catch on to... What was the name of that guy who proposed to her a few months after your dad died?" She snapped her fingers. "Stanley something, wasn't it?"

The question hit like a body blow. "Are you talking about Stanley Chinsky?"

She hesitated, reacting to his tone. "Um. Did he head Piretti's accounting department at some point?"

"Yes. He was also a board member." Outrage filled him. "That bastard had the nerve to propose to Mom?"

Catherine made a production of sliding her can into one of the drink holders, her gaze flitting away from his. "I gather she never mentioned it."

"No, she didn't."

Catherine released a gusty sigh. "I'm sorry, Gabe. I didn't realize or I'd never have said anything. She told me about it that night we had our heart-to-heart."

"Did she also tell you that Stanley attempted to rob her blind during his tenure as our accountant?"

"Actually, she did. I think she blamed herself to some extent," Catherine offered. "She thought her refusal of his proposal may have provoked his retaliation."

"The hell it did. He started stealing from us the minute my father died. If he proposed to her, it was only in the hopes of covering up his little scheme."

Catherine offered a tentative smile. "Dina did say it was a pretty clever one."

"It was. It took me forever to figure out—" He broke off. "Son of a bitch. Son of a *bitch*. Why the hell didn't I see it?"

"See what?"

He turned on her. "This is your fault, you know. If I hadn't been so distracted by you, I'd have seen it right off."

"Damn it, Gabe. Seen *what?*"

"What my mother's been up to." He turned the boat in a wide arc and goosed the throttle. "The reason you're going bankrupt is that my dear mother has been skimming the accounts."

Nine

It took several hours for Gabe and Catherine to work their way back from Lake Washington to Shilshole Bay and safely dock the boat at the marina. They arrived on Dina's doorstep just as dusk settled over the city. She opened the door with a wide smile, one that faded the instant she got a good look at their expressions.

She stepped back to allow them in. "I'm busted, aren't I?"

"Oh, yeah," Gabe confirmed. "Seriously busted."

Her chin shot up. "Actually, I expected this confrontation quite a bit sooner. I'm a little disappointed in you, Gabriel."

"And you'd have gotten this confrontation sooner if I hadn't been so distracted by Catherine."

Dina nodded. "I have to admit, I was counting on that."

They stood in the foyer, the three of them as awkward and uncomfortable as strangers. Gabe thrust a hand through his hair. "What the hell is going on, Mom? How could you do such a thing to Catherine? She trusted you, and you betrayed that trust."

In response, Catherine eased her hand over the tensed muscles of his arm. "There's a good reason, Gabe. There has to be."

Dina smiled her approval. "Why don't I make a pot of coffee while we chat?"

"Chat." Gabe stared at her in disbelief. "This isn't some sort of afternoon social. Coffee's not going to fix this. This is serious. This is jail-time serious."

An expression not unlike Gabe's settled over her face, one of ruthless determination. "If you want your questions answered, then we'll do it over coffee. Because I'm not saying another word, otherwise."

He turned to Catherine. "I'm sorry about this. I swear I had no idea."

She simply shook her head. "Let's hear her out."

Dina linked her arm through Catherine's and drew her toward the kitchen. "Don't worry," she whispered. "It's not as bad as it seems."

"No, it's worse," Gabe broke in, clearly overhearing. "You and Stanley can have adjoining cells."

"Catherine isn't going to turn me over to the authorities," Dina replied with calm certainty. "Not after I explain."

"This better be one hell of a good explanation."

Dina made short work of the coffee. The entire time, she chatted about anything and everything except the reason they were there. Pouring coffee into mugs, she carried them to the table. "You both have had some sun today," she commented, spooning sugar into her cup. "It's nice to see that you're spending so much time together and working things out between you."

"Mom." Just that one word. Quiet. Fighting for patience. But with an underlying demand she couldn't mistake.

She gave her teaspoon an irritable tap against the porcelain edge of the mug and released her breath in a sigh. "All right, fine. Ask your questions."

Gabe reached for Catherine's hand and gave it a reassuring squeeze. "You skimmed money out of the Elegant Events accounts." He didn't phrase it as a question.

"Yes, I did." Dina leaned back in her chair and took a sip of coffee. "I'm sorry, Catherine, but you made it quite easy. I highly recommend you take a few accounting courses so no one else takes advantage of you in the future."

Catherine lifted an eyebrow and to Gabe's disbelief, he caught a hint of amusement at his mother's outrageous suggestion. Though what she could find amusing about any of this he had no idea. "Why, thank you for your advice, Dina. I'll get right on that," she murmured.

Gabe stepped in again. "You used the Chinsky method, I assume."

"Oh, yes. Stanley was an excellent teacher. I just

followed his example and did to Catherine precisely what he'd done to me." She shrugged. "And then I waited."

This time, he reached for his mother's hand. "Are you hurting for money? Has something happened that you've been afraid to tell me? Whatever it is, I'll do everything in my power to help. You know that, don't you?"

Tears welled up in Dina's eyes. "Oh, Gabriel. You have no idea how much your saying that means to me. You've always done your best to look out for me." She gave him a misty smile. "But it's not about the money, dear."

"Then, what?" Catherine asked. She caught her lip between her teeth. "Is this because I left Gabe? Is this some sort of payback?"

Dina inhaled sharply. "You think I did this out of revenge? Oh, no, sweetheart. Never that. I love you as though you were my own daughter. How could you doubt that?" Her gaze, bird bright, shifted from Gabe to Catherine. "No, I did it to help the two of you."

"To help us," Catherine repeated, confusion overriding every other emotion. "How does driving our business into bankruptcy help?"

"Think about it. What did you do once you realized we were having financial difficulties?"

"I tried to drum up more business. I economized. I worked to reduce overhead and increase—" She broke off and closed her eyes. "Of course. I went to Gabe."

"There you go." Dina patted her hand. "I knew you'd get there eventually. Just as I knew that if our finances became serious enough and you couldn't see any other option available to you, you'd eventually go and ask Gabriel for help. I have to tell you, I was quite impressed by your determination not to give in. I almost had to scrap the entire plan."

"But I caved before you had to."

She beamed. "Exactly."

"Are you telling me," Gabe gritted out, "that you set up this entire scam, put Catherine through hell and back, as a matchmaking scheme?"

Dina tilted her head to one side in a mannerism identical to Gabe's. "I'd say that pretty much covers it, yes. And it worked, didn't it? You two are back together and looking happier than ever. If I hadn't stepped in, you'd still be apart and miserable." She tapped her index finger against the tabletop. "And before you lose that infamous Piretti temper of yours, let me tell you that I'd have done almost anything, risked just about any consequence in order to give you the opportunity to work out your differences. You taught me that, Gabriel, when you abducted me. You didn't care what ultimately happened to you as a result of your actions, so long as we patched up our relationship."

Gabe wrestled his temper under control, with only limited success. "I believe the expression is…hoisted by my own petard." And didn't that just bite? Another thought occurred to him. "And are you also behind the sabotage of her reputation?"

Dina's mug hit the table with a crack. "Absolutely not. How can you think I'd do such a thing?"

"Oh, hell, Mom. I don't know. Maybe because you stole from her?"

She sniffed. "That's different. The money didn't actually go anywhere. It's safe and sound. Catherine's name is even on the account where I have the funds stashed. So, technically, it probably isn't embezzlement."

"Technically, when I kill you it won't be murder because there's not a man alive who wouldn't consider it justifiable momicide." Okay, so maybe his temper wasn't totally under control.

"That's enough, Gabe," Catherine said, stepping into the fray. "It's time to go."

For the first time, Dina's smile faltered. "Are you terribly angry with me? I really was trying to help."

To Gabe's surprise, Catherine left her chair and crouched beside Dina. She wrapped her arms around the older woman and whispered something in her ear, something he couldn't make out. All he knew was that it made his mother cry, though a single look told him they were tears of happiness. Then Catherine straightened and glanced at Gabe.

"Could you take me back to your apartment, please?" she asked.

Not home, he noted. But to *his* apartment. He could feel the time remaining between them growing short, could almost hear the clock ticking down the final minutes, and his jaw clenched. Now that he'd resolved Catherine's financial issues, and her reputation had regained its footing, he was rapidly running out of leverage for convincing her to stay with him. Did she want to return to his place because she planned to pack up and return to her apartment?

If so, he'd better come up with a new plan for convincing her to stay…and fast.

Gabe's tension was palpable the entire drive to his place and Catherine didn't dare say a word in case it was the wrong word, one that set off whatever was building inside him. She waited quietly while he inserted his key in the lock and shoved open the door, allowing her to enter ahead of him.

The interior lay in utter darkness and thundering silence, a silence broken only by the harsh sound of their breathing. She switched on the lamp by the wooden sculpture of the sleeping woman and trailed her hand along the fluid lines. It had become a habit to caress the small statue whenever she entered the apartment.

"I bought that after you left because it reminded me of you," Gabe said.

"Does it?" She took another look. She couldn't see the similarity herself, but then she had no idea what she looked like when asleep. She could only hope it was this graceful. "Why would you do that when our relationship was over?"

"Because it wasn't over. It isn't over."

She couldn't miss the implacable tone, the underlying statement that he planned to do everything within his power to convince her to stay, even after all the problems at Elegant Events had been resolved. And he was right. It wasn't over between them.

Not yet. Not tonight.

"And when our business is concluded?" She glanced at him over her shoulder. He stood in shadow, making it impossible to read his expression. But there was no mistaking the look in his eyes. A look of utter ruthlessness. "You aren't going to honor your promise and let me go, are you?"

"No."

She nodded to herself. "I didn't think so."

In a single supple movement she snagged the hem of her T-shirt and pulled it up over her head. The scrap of cotton fluttered to the floor, a pale flag of surrender against the gray carpet.

"What are you doing?" The question escaped, abrasive as sandpaper.

She unsnapped her shorts and shimmied out of them, letting them pool at her feet before stepping clear of them. "What does it look like I'm doing?"

"It looks remarkably like a striptease." He reached for her, but she evaded him. "Why, Catherine?"

Reaching behind her, she unhooked her bathing suit top and let it slip away into the darkness. "Why am I taking off my clothes? Why aren't I packing up and moving out? Or why did you never come after me when I left? Why did your mother have to go to such extremes to throw us together again?"

He ignored all her questions, but one. "Are you staying?"

She hooked her thumbs in the scrap of silk anchored to her hips and slid it off. She headed for the bedroom, turning at the last minute to say, "It would be a shame to let all Dina's hard work go to waste, wouldn't it?"

He caught up with her in the hallway. Without a word, he swept her high into his arms and carried her into the bedroom. The world spun dizzily around her right before the bed reached up to cushion their fall. Still he didn't speak. But she found that words weren't necessary. Not when he said it all in a single kiss.

His mouth closed over hers, first in tender benediction, then in something else. She sensed he wanted to be gentle, but this wasn't a night for gentleness. Something fierce and desperate and raw erupted between them. It was as though they'd been stripped to their bare essence, all polish and sophistication shredded, with only an elemental need remaining.

"I can't hold back tonight," he said in between kisses.

"I don't want you to."

He gathered her up and spread her across the silk bedcover, anchoring her wrists above her head with one hand while shaping her lean contours with the other. And then he feasted on what her striptease had bared. His mouth captured her breast. While the light nip and tug shot her skyward, his hand slid to her hip and then through the crisp triangle of curls. He cupped her, and with one slow, torturous stroke with his clever, clever fingers he had her erupting.

"No," she moaned. "I want more. I want you."

"And you'll have me," he promised. "Patience, sweetheart."

"You be patient. I'll have you now."

She fought free of his hold and pushed at his shoulders, rolling him onto his back. He didn't put up much of a struggle, but then she didn't expect him to. It was her turn to explore. Her turn to taste, then devour. Her turn to sculpt lines as graceful as the wooden statue he'd compared her to. But his lines flowed with a far different type of grace. His body was hard and crisp and honed. And utterly, gloriously male.

She started at the top of him, with that face that was just a shade too pretty for his own good. Sooty brows. Eyes of cobalt blue that pierced mere skin and bone and arrowed right through to the heart and soul of her. A nose, straight and proud. His jaw, a stubborn block of granite that once set could rarely be shifted. And his mouth.

She fell into his mouth, moaning at the endless sweep and parry of his tongue that never failed to send her heart tripping and racing like a sprinter's. And still, it wasn't enough. More, more, more. She wanted to explore every single inch and give to him the way he'd so often given to her.

His throat moved convulsively as she kissed her way along it and she could feel a harsh groan building there, rumbling against her lips. "Not in control now, are we, Piretti?" she teased. "Looks like there's a new pirate in charge of the pillaging and plundering."

"Pillage any more of my plunder and I'll go digging for your buried treasure."

She choked on a laugh and skittered downward. "Not yet. I have other plans for you first."

Like his amazing chest. It had driven her crazy the entire day, watching him helm his yacht in just a pair of white gauze, drawstring pants slung low on his narrow hips. He truly had a spectacular physique, with powerful arms roped with muscle and yards of deeply tanned, lightly furred chest. And when he'd bent down to adjust one of the boat fenders or secure the lines, the sight of his tight, rounded flanks almost brought her to her knees. All she could think about throughout those endless hours was giving that drawstring of his a little jerk. Now she could.

She made quick work of it, loosening the waistband and delving inside. She followed the plunging line of crisp, dark hair until she hit her own personal treasure. He felt hot to the touch, that peculiar combination of sleek overlying steel one that never failed to amaze, even as it aroused. She wanted to give to him, give something special. So first she touched; then she tasted.

The groan finally escaped his throat, an eruption of sound, followed by an eruption of movement. He dragged her upward, flipped her, and with a single swift plunge mated them one to the other. Energy shot through her, a tense expectation that hovered just out of reach.

"I'm sorry." The words were torn from him. "I'm so sorry."

She cupped his face, forcing that wild blue gaze to fix on her. "Why are you sorry? How can you possibly be sorry when we're here, together, like this?"

"My mother was wrong to force you into this. I was wrong to force you."

Catherine could barely hang on. "This isn't wrong." It was perfect. It was heaven on earth. "It never was and never could be."

The breath burned from his lungs. "You didn't take her apart as you had every right to do. I don't know what you said to her, but it made her so happy."

In a smooth flow of movement, Catherine cinched his waist with her legs and pulled him in tight. "You want to know what I said?" She gave herself up to his helpless movements, caught the rhythm with him and rode the storm. "I told her thank you."

They shattered then, falling apart in each other's arms. Catherine stared blindly up at him, knowing that she'd never be able to gather up all the pieces again, never be able to put them together the way they were before. She'd done the unthinkable that day.

She'd fallen in love with Gabe again.

"Why did you leave me?"

In the exhausted fallout from their lovemaking, the question caught her completely off guard and utterly defenseless. No doubt he'd planned it that way. "Do we have to do this now?"

He rolled over to face her and lifted onto an elbow. His expression was so serious, so determined. "Something happened, didn't it?"

"Yes."

"Something more than my giving work priority at the worst possible time."

"Yes," she whispered again.

"What happened?"

"Please, Gabe. Tonight was so special, I don't want anything to ruin it. I owe you the truth. I know I do. And I'll give it to you, I promise."

He swept wayward curls from her face, his gaze one of infinite compassion. "You thought this moment wouldn't come, didn't you? That our relationship would fall apart and spare you whatever it is you need to confess."

"Yes." She sat up and snagged the sheet, wrapping it around herself. It was a telling gesture. She took a minute to think through her options, aware of him tamping down on his impatience so she had that opportunity. "Do you know what the weekend after next is?"

She could see he didn't care for the abrupt change in subject. "What's that got to do with anything?"

"The date," she continued doggedly. "Do you know the significance of the date?"

He paused to consider, then nodded. "It'll be two years to the day that you left."

"I want you to take four days off—just four days—and go away with me that weekend. You choose the spot. Someplace special."

He left the bed, his movements uncharacteristically jerky. "Are you serious?"

"Quite serious. If you'll do that, I'll answer any and all questions you put to me. And I'll answer them unconditionally." She hesitated. "But I think I should warn you that you're not going to like what you hear."

He snagged a pair of jeans and yanked them on. He'd never looked more potently male than in that moment.

His hair was rumpled from their lovemaking, and traces of fierce passion still cut across the planes of his face. Even his body was taut and scented with aggression. The predator had escaped from beneath his civilized cloak and he was on the prowl.

"Why all the drama, Catherine? Why not just come clean here and now?"

She looked around with wistful affection. "I don't want any more ghosts haunting this place than there already are. And I want to deal with our issues on neutral territory. Either we're able to put it all behind us and move on." She swallowed. "Or we call it quits."

"Son of a—" He thrust a hand through his hair. "You think next weekend is going to end our relationship, don't you?"

A vise tightened around her throat, and she had to force out her answer. "Yes. Please, Gabe. I want—I need—this time beforehand."

"All right, fine. I'll arrange to take that weekend off and give you the time you're asking." He stalked toward the bed. Perhaps it was his partial nudity. Perhaps it was the distracting gap in his jeans. Perhaps it was simply that he still had a prowl to his step. Whatever the cause, she'd never seen him more intimidating. "But hear me, Catherine, and hear me well. I won't let you go. Whatever this secret is, we'll work our way through it."

"I want to believe that."

He rested a knee on the mattress and cupped her face. "All you have to do is let me in. All you have to do is trust me. I'm not going to walk away from you. We will figure this out, after which I'm going to propose to you again. And this time I won't let anything interfere. No phone calls. No business. And no secrets."

Tears overflowed, spilling with helpless abandon down her cheeks. "I'm afraid."

"I know you are." He feathered a kiss across her mouth. "But there's nothing I can do about that, no way to reassure you, until you're honest with me."

The next several days passed as though on wings. With each one that slipped away, Catherine saw the death of her dreams approach with lightning-fast speed. Her days became overloaded with work, necessary if she was going to take the next weekend off to be with Gabe. But the nights…

Seated at the small desk in her bedroom, Catherine set her current checklist aside as she paused to consider. The nights overflowed with a passion unlike anything that had gone before. It was as though Gabe were determined to put some indelible mark on her, to prove that what existed between them could never be lost. Would never end.

But all things ended.

She shivered at the thought, then forced herself to return to work, scanning the checklist for any minor details she might have overlooked. At her elbow, the phone rang and she picked up the receiver. "Catherine Haile," she said, still focused more on work than the caller.

"May I speak with Mr. Gabe Piretti, please?" The voice was young, female and friendly.

"I'm sorry, he's not available," Catherine said absentmindedly. "May I take a message?"

"Hmm. Maybe you can help me. This is Theresa from Très Romantique. I'm calling regarding the reservations he made with us."

Catherine put down her checklist and perked up a little. "Actually, I can help you with that."

"Lovely." Relief sounded in her voice. "When Mr. Piretti originally booked with us, he requested a suite."

"Did he?" Catherine murmured, pleased by his thoughtfulness.

"But when he changed the dates, the room was switched from a suite to a standard king. I took Mr. Piretti's original reservations myself, and I remember how adamant he was about wanting that particular suite. So, before I let it go, I just want to double-check that my associate didn't misunderstand his request." Theresa lowered her voice. "She's new, and I'm in charge of training her, so it's my head if a mistake is made. Besides, it would be a shame for him to lose that room, if it's the one he actually wanted. It's absolutely gorgeous."

Catherine frowned. "I'm sorry. Run that by me again. He changed the dates? We're not booked for this next weekend?"

"No, ma'am. It's been switched to one week later. One moment, please.…" A muffled conversation ensued and then Theresa came back onto the line. "Kaisy says she remembers something about a work conflict. Fortunately, due to a recent cancelation, that particular suite is available both weekends. So if you could just confirm which room we should be holding…?"

The hell with which room. Right now all that mattered

was which date. "Theresa, could I get back to you on that?" Catherine asked as calmly as she could manage. "I need a few hours to check into it."

"I'm afraid I can't hold the suite past five today," she explained. "Would that give you sufficient time?"

"That will be fine," Catherine replied. "Thank you for calling."

She returned the receiver to its cradle using the greatest of care, and closed her eyes while despair swamped her. How could Gabe make that change without consulting her first? He knew. He knew how important this weekend was to her, that she'd planned to speak frankly about what had happened two years ago. Why would he undermine all that?

They'd grown so close over the past month. They'd finally learned to trust, had slowly, but surely, dealt with their differences. She'd witnessed the change in him. Understood why Piretti's was of such importance to him, just as he'd accepted the importance of her career. And this was what it came down to.

When everything was said and done, all his fine promises to reorganize his priorities were just so much talk. He hadn't changed, not really.

She fought for calm as she considered her options. Last time she'd run. Last time she'd been ill and her only thought had been to hide somewhere safe while she licked her wounds. But she wasn't the same woman she'd been two years ago. Catherine shoved back her chair and stood.

This time she'd fight back.

Ten

Catherine had little memory of the drive across town to Piretti's headquarters. Little memory of parking her car in the underground lot, or taking the elevator straight to the top using the special coded key card Gabe had given her that allowed her direct access to the highest of the high.

She only woke to her surroundings as she strode, rapid-fire, across the plush carpet toward Gabe's office. Roxanne sat at her desk, smiling that smug smile of hers, and it took every ounce of self-control not to ball up a fist and plant it right in that pouty red mouth. Did she know? Catherine couldn't help but wonder. Did that explain the delighted look in her eye, one that said she would relish every minute of the scene about to unfold?

She swept past Roxanne's desk and thrust open Gabe's door without so much as a perfunctory knock. He was in a meeting, not that she gave a damn. She slammed the door closed behind her.

"Did you cancel our plans for this weekend?" she demanded.

Everyone froze. All eyes swiveled from her to Gabe. "Gentlemen…" He jerked his head toward the door. "Clear the decks."

There was a minor scrambling toward the exit, like rats deserting a sinking ship. The last man overboard pulled the door shut behind him as gently as though it were made of Waterford crystal. Catherine knew she was handling this badly, but she was too furious to care. She tossed her purse onto the chair in front of Gabe's desk, considered sitting and elected to stand. Gabe rose to confront her. Annoyance, bordering on anger, glittered in his blue eyes.

"What's going on, Catherine?"

To her horror she felt tears pressing into her throat and behind her eyelids. She'd planned to maintain her cool, to use a hint of self-righteous anger to carry her through a difficult conversation. Instead, she could feel herself crumbling. She balled her hands into fists, and fought for control.

"I had a phone call less than an hour ago from Très Romantique informing me that you'd called and changed our reservations from this week to next due to a work conflict." Her control wobbled, but she fought back. "I know you probably don't think there's any difference between one week and another. But it mattered—*matters*—to me. I thought you understood." She looked him dead in the eye so there'd be no mistaking her feelings on the matter. "So, here's the bottom line. When I need you, I need you. It can't always be at your convenience. Sometimes life happens and it ends up happening during a meeting or during a negotiation or...or—" To her horror, her voice broke.

"Catherine—"

She waved him off. "No!" She snatched a quick, calming breath, relieved to feel the press of tears ease just enough for her to speak. "No, Gabe. Things have changed. *I've* changed. I'm not handling our little crisis the way I did two years ago. I'm not going to remain silent any longer. I'm not going to sit by the phone waiting for your call. I'm not going to leave you a note. And I'm damn sure not going to run. This time I'll have my say."

Some indefinable reaction shifted across his expression, one she couldn't take the time to analyze, not if she wanted to get through this.

"I'm listening."

But for how long? And how would it ultimately affect their relationship? "I don't care if this weekend interferes with business issues. I need you. Not last weekend. Not the weekend after. *This* weekend."

"Why?" he asked quietly.

She simply stood and stared at him, her grief and sorrow leaking from her in an unstoppable stream. "The date."

"It's the two-year anniversary of the date you left me. I got that part."

She caught a glimpse of the emotion behind that subtle shift in expression, a hint of anger combined with a wealth of pain.

"What I haven't been able to figure is why you'd want to go out of your way to commemorate the occasion."

She could feel the blood drain from her face. "Commemorate? You thought—" Oh, no. No, no, no. "Oh, Gabe, that's not it at all. I'm so sorry you thought so. I don't want to commemorate it."

His eyes closed briefly and he swore beneath his breath. "Aw, hell. You planned to replace the memories, didn't you?" Circling the desk, he pulled her close, and with that one simple touch, the fury and tension drained away. He cupped her face and turned it up to his. "You're attempting to superimpose new memories, happy memories over top of what went before."

She stared at him, her chin trembling. "How could you think otherwise?"

He gave a half-humorous shrug. "It happens. And it's going to happen again, especially when we miss a small step…such as the one where you explain your plan in advance."

She was an idiot. She'd assumed he'd understand without her having to go there. "Sometimes I forget you don't read minds." She let the sigh pour out of her.

"Is that why, Gabe? Is that why you changed the date? You thought I planned to rub salt in the wound? Is that really something you believe I'd do?"

"Listen carefully, Catherine…." He lowered his head and feathered a brief kiss across her mouth. "I. Didn't. Change. The. Date."

It took her a moment to process the words. "But…but I had a phone call from Theresa at Très Romantique. She said you did."

"She's mistaken." He edged his hip onto his desk and reached for his PDA. "Let's get this straightened out, shall we?"

Tapping with the stylus, he brought up the information he needed and then placed a call. A few minutes later he was connected to Reservations. It never ceased to amaze her how cleanly he managed to cut straight through to the heart of the matter, explaining the problem in a few short sentences. He listened for a while to what Catherine could only presume was Theresa's chronicle of events.

"Got it. I'll be certain to tell your manager how much I appreciate your thoughtfulness in calling about the suite, especially since it's clear that the error was on my end. I also appreciate your reinstating the original reservation. In the meantime, could you check with Kaisy and ask her specifically who changed the date? Not at all. I'll wait."

His gaze shifted to Catherine and she shivered. She'd only seen that look in his eye once before, when he'd discovered an employee had been cheating him. She never forgot that particular expression, just as she hoped never to see it again.

"Thank you, Theresa. That's precisely what I needed." He disconnected the call and then punched a button on his desk phone. "Roxanne, would you step into my office for a moment?"

Catherine released her breath in a slow sigh. Of course. How incredibly foolish of her not to have suspected as much. You could paint a leopard purple, but there were still spots lurking under all that dye. Roxanne could no more change her character than a leopard could change from a predator to a rabbit, regardless of threats and coercion.

How it must have chafed to toe the line. And when the opportunity arose to try for one more bit of mischief, she probably found it too much to resist. One more petty little slap, especially if she sensed how much it would hurt. Another thought occurred. Maybe she believed that Catherine couldn't change her spots, either. Maybe she thought that history would repeat itself, and Catherine would run, rather than tackle the problem head-on.

She and Gabe both waited in silence until Roxanne slithered into the room. Catherine scrutinized her closely. Today she'd chosen to project a far different image. She wore a beautiful ivory high-neck dress with tiny pearl buttons down the fitted bodice. A demure touch of lace gave the dress an almost bridal appearance. The entire ensemble was reminiscent of the turn of the previous century, right down to the Gibson Girl manner in which she'd piled her hair on top of her head. She carried a steno pad and pen, held at the ready.

"How can I help you, Gabe?" she asked sweetly.

"Answer a question for me, Roxanne."

She kept her dark gaze trained on her boss, completely ignoring Catherine. "Of course." She smiled, projecting the perfect amount of flirtatious innocence. "Anything at all. You know that."

"I had a reservation at Très Romantique. It's been changed. Do you know anything about it?"

"I do," she responded calmly. "I was going to tell you about it after your meeting ended, but…" She shot Catherine a swift, chiding glance. "I hadn't counted on Ms. Haile disrupting things."

He forced her back on point. "Explain what happened with the reservation."

"Certainly. I had a call from Mr. LaRue. He said that he had some sort of scheduling conflict and that Wednesday was no longer convenient to sign the final contracts. He insisted we change it."

"Insisted?"

She sighed. "Oh, Gabe, you know how he can be. He was adamant. I did my best to change his mind, but he wouldn't be budged. Only one other date would do and that happened to be during those days you had me block off. When I argued, he said it was then or never." She shook her head in distress. "What could I do? I told him I'd check with you and then thought maybe I could help you avert a blowup with Catherine by calling Très Romantique to see if they had any availability for the following week. I'm so sorry I failed. Clearly, Catherine isn't open to compromise."

"You canceled my reservations without checking with me first?"

She hesitated for a split second. "Of course not. I explained the conflict and had the girl hold the room for both dates. She agreed to do so until I had a chance to check with you." Her eyes widened. "Oh, no. Don't tell me she didn't do as I asked?"

"The girl's name is Kaisy. And that's not how she remembers the conversation going down."

Catherine had to give Roxanne credit. She didn't react to the comment by so much as a flicker of an eyelash. Nor did she deviate from her story. If anything her shock and indignation increased. "Then this Kaisy misunderstood. Either that or she's trying to cover up her mistake."

Gabe smiled. "Well, that explains that," he said smoothly.

Roxanne relaxed ever so slightly, even daring to shoot Catherine the tiniest of looks from the corner of her eye, one glowing with triumph. "Is there anything else?"

"I think there might be. Just give me a minute." He picked up the phone and stabbed out another number. "Gabe Piretti here," he replied to whatever greeting he received. "Is the big man around? Yes, I would, thanks."

Another brief pause. "Jack? I'm putting you on speaker, is that all right?"

"Sure...." His voice boomed into the room. "Not another change to our meeting, I hope?"

"Actually, that's why I'm calling."

Gabe fixed his eyes on his assistant, pinning her in place. She turned ashen. The shade clashed with her pretty little ivory dress, Catherine decided. Not at all a good color combination for her. She should have stuck with jewel tones. Besides, ivory was just going to draw attention to the boot print about to be inflicted to her curvaceous derriere.

"I'm looking at a note that Roxanne left me about the change to our meeting date," Gabe continued. "Was our original time inconvenient?"

"Hell, no. Roxy said it was bad for you."

Roxanne opened her mouth to interrupt and with one vicious look, Gabe had the words dying before they were ever spoken. "That's what she told you? That I wanted it changed?"

"Yup. Had it right from those sweet luscious lips of hers. I have to admit, I wasn't too happy about it. If she weren't so pretty with her apology, I would have raised holy hell."

"And why's that, Jack?"

"Because I was planning on ditching town the minute I cashed your check. Had a nice little vacation all planned out to kick off my retirement. Wife's none too pleased, either. Hasn't stopped pecking at me since I broke the news to her."

"I'll tell you what, Jack. Let me make a few adjustments at this end so you can go ahead and keep those plans. I wouldn't want to upset Marie."

"That's damn decent of you, Gabe. Think I'll tell her I ripped you a new one and you agreed to switch it back. You don't mind if I make myself the hero of the piece, do you?"

"Go right ahead. My best to Marie, and I'll see you Wednesday, as originally planned." He cut the connection. "You're fired, Roxanne. I've just buzzed for security. They'll help you clear out your desk. Then they will escort you to payroll, where I'll have a two-month severance check cut for you."

"Please, Gabe," she said in a soft, penitent undertone. "Don't I get a chance to explain?"

He didn't hesitate. "No." Hard. Cold. Absolute. "You stood here in front of me, looked me dead in the eye and lied. You changed those dates for one reason and one reason only. To hit out at Catherine. No one does that to my woman and gets away with it."

"If you'd just let me explain," she pleaded, huge tears welling up in her eyes, "you'd see this is just a big misunderstanding."

"You're right. My misunderstanding. I knew what you were when I hired you. I thought I could use that to my advantage. But I'd forgotten the cardinal rule. If you pick up a snake, expect to get bitten."

The tears dried and fury replaced her contrition. "I'll sue you. If you fire me, I'll sue you for every dime you have."

Gabe slowly climbed to his feet. "Try it, Roxanne. Please. I want you to. I'm asking you to." That gave her pause, and he smiled. "You were getting the axe today, no matter what."

"*What?*" Roxanne and Catherine asked in unison.

He spared Catherine a brief glance. "You should have told me, right from the start, and spared us both two years' worth of grief." Then he returned his attention to Roxanne. "I did a little digging into what happened at the Marconi party. And the strangest thing kept happening. Your name kept coming up. So you go right ahead and make your next call to a lawyer. Make sure he's a really good one. Because my next call is to the King County Sheriff's Department. And just so you know, unlike Catherine, I play hardball. I will see to it that her name and reputation are restored and that you are forced to take responsibility for your actions."

Without a word, Roxanne spun on her heel and forged a swift path across his office. She'd barely reached the door when Gabe stopped her. "Once you get your legal issues straightened out, I suggest you consider a fresh start somewhere else, Roxanne. Someplace far out of my reach." He let that sink in before adding, "And just so you know, I have a long, long reach."

She swung around at that, aiming her vindictiveness straight at Catherine, where she knew it would do the most damage. "You may think you've won, but you haven't. Not when he finds out the truth. When he discovers you're damaged goods, he'll end your affair."

Then she switched her gaze to Gabe. "I did a little digging of my own. Placed a few phone calls. Maybe pretended to be someone I wasn't in order to get all the juicy tidbits I needed. Has your lovely bride-to-be warned you that she can't have children? If you marry her, it's the end of your branch of the precious Piretti line. I hope you two have a really great life." And with that, she slammed from the room.

Silence reigned for an endless moment. Catherine stood, frozen in place. She had to say something. Anything. But it was just a fight to continue breathing. The ability to speak was a sheer impossibility.

"Catherine?"

She shook her head and held up a hand in an effort to fend him off. Not that it stopped him. He crossed to her side and, catching her off guard, scooped her up into his arms and carried her to the sitting area by the windows. There he lowered her onto the couch and followed her down, aligning their bodies one to the other. Catherine had no idea how long he held her, murmuring words of comfort and sharing his warmth until the trembling gradually eased.

"I'm sorry, Gabe," she said at last. "I should have told you right from the start."

"She wasn't lying, was she?"

Catherine shook her head. "I can't have this conversation. Not like this. Not with you touching me." She tried to push him away, attempted to put some small amount of distance between them. Not that it worked. "Gabe, please. I can't do this."

But he didn't listen. If anything, he held her closer. Put his hands on her. Warmed her. And refused to let her go. "Shh. It's all right, sweetheart."

"No! No, it's not all right. It'll never be all right."

"What happened? Tell me what happened."

She caved, shrinking into herself. She couldn't put this off any longer. Couldn't hide from the truth, no matter how badly she wanted to. Time to face him and end it. Time to finally and completely face it herself. Time to shatter both their worlds. "It was the night you proposed," she said dully. "You asked me to marry you and I was going to tell you something, remember?"

"I remember."

"I was going to tell you I was pregnant with our child. I'd been hugging the secret to myself for two full weeks, waiting for the right time."

He went rigid in her arms. And she saw those gorgeous eyes light up with almost boyish wonder and excitement. Then the light extinguished as realization set in. "Oh, God. Something went wrong. What happened? Was there an accident?"

Exhaustion filled her. "Not an accident, no. The doctors said it was a spontaneous abortion. Something was wrong with the fetus. I lost the baby." Her voice cracked. "Oh, Gabe. I lost our baby."

He cradled her close and simply held her, waiting out the tears. "Was Roxanne right? Are you unable to have more children?"

"I don't know how she found out. Who knows?

Maybe she called the doctor and posed as me. I wouldn't put anything past her."

"Catherine, please. What happened?"

She'd avoided answering his question and they both knew it. But the time had come to give it to him straight. "The 'how' doesn't matter, does it? The bottom line is, yes. She's right. I can never have children. I was crazed after I lost the baby. That's when I left you. But the bleeding wouldn't stop." Her face crumpled. "A few days later I had to have a partial hysterectomy."

He hugged her close. "I'm sorry. I'm so sorry, Cate. That's what you meant when you said you were broken."

"Did I say that?" She couldn't remember.

He closed his eyes and leaned into her. "Oh, Christ, honey. Where the hell was I when you were going through all that? It was that damn lawsuit, wasn't it?"

"I called you from the hospital," she offered softly. "I'm guessing you didn't receive any of the messages."

"No." Just that one word. But it said it all.

"Do you understand now why I would only agree to a temporary affair?"

He tensed. "Don't tell me you buy in to Roxanne's load of crap."

"She didn't say anything I hadn't already realized for myself."

He raised himself up onto an elbow so he could scrutinize her expression. "You think I'd end our relationship because you can't have children? You think I wouldn't marry you tomorrow because of it? Are you kidding me? Do you honestly think so little of me?"

"You've always wanted a big family," she stated unevenly. "We had endless discussions about it. Piretti's has been in your family for generations. You want children to carry on the name."

"Right, so?"

"So we can't have children!"

"Yes, Catherine, we can. It's called adoption."

"But they wouldn't be your flesh and blood."

That drove him from her arms. "What the hell kind of a man do you take me for? Do you really think me so shallow?"

She stared mutely, shaking her head.

He snatched a deep breath and gathered up his self-control. "Tell me something, sweetheart. Do you need to have a child grow in your womb for you to love and raise a baby as though it were your own?"

"No, but—"

"Neither do I. Neither does any man on this planet, since we don't bear children."

"I do know my basic biology, Gabe."

"I'm relieved to hear it. Think, Cate. Men can't experience what women do during those nine months they carry a child. And yet we bond with our baby when it's born, even though it didn't come directly from our own bodies. How is that any different from what will happen when we adopt?"

She shook her head again, unable to answer. Afraid to believe.

"And what if this had happened after we married? Do you think me the sort of man who would divorce you because of it?"

She started to cry then. How could she love this man so dearly and not have seen the truth? Not have seen all the way to the very heart of him? How could she have given Roxanne so much power? It wasn't Gabe who was guilty of not having enough faith. She was the one to blame.

"I'm sorry, Gabe. I should have trusted you."

"I won't argue that point. But I didn't give you a lot of reason to trust me, not while I had my priorities so screwed up."

For the first time in two long years, she could see clearly. "If I'd come to you about Roxanne two years ago, you'd have fired her then, wouldn't you?"

"Yes. I had no idea she'd become such a problem for you, or she would have been replaced within the hour."

Now for her biggest concern. "Where do we go from here?" she asked.

"That's an excellent question." He returned to the couch and took her into his arms, rolled on top of her so she was deliciously cushioned beneath him. "First off, we keep our weekend reservation at Très Romantique."

A small smile crept across Catherine's mouth and she could feel the beginnings of something precious sprouting inside her. Hope. Hope was taking hold and putting down roots. Deep, unshakable roots. "And then?"

"Then we make sure we've cleared away every last

secret, every last doubt and every last concern while I explain to you, slowly and clearly, just how much I love you."

She threw her arms around him and held on for all she was worth. "I love you desperately, Gabe."

He closed his eyes and she felt his tension drain away. "You have no idea how long I've waited to hear those words again."

And then he kissed her. It was a soft caress, unexpectedly gentle. A benediction. A promise. He kept it simple, the passion tempered and muted. And yet it was a kiss Catherine would remember for the rest of her life. It melded them, heart and mind, body and soul. With that one kiss, all doubts faded, replaced by certainty. This was her man, just as she was his woman. Whatever the future brought, they'd face it together.

It was a long time before Gabe spoke again. "After we have everything settled between us, I'll need to speak with someone at Elegant Events." He shot her a wicked grin. "I have it on good authority that they're the best event stager in town."

A smile flirted with Catherine's mouth. "As a matter of fact, they are."

"I'll need to speak to their top event specialist," he warned.

"I happen to know she has a very busy calendar. But she might find room for Gabe 'the Pirate' Piretti. If he asked nicely." She tilted her head to one side. "Tell me. What would you need with a top-notch event specialist?"

"I need her to plan the wedding of the year."

"Why, Mr. Piretti," she protested indignantly. "That sounds like you're asking me to mix business with pleasure. I thought we had rules about that sort of thing."

"The hell with the rules."

She pretended to look scandalized. "No more strictly business?"

He shook his head. "From now on you are my business—first, last, and foremost."

And he proceeded to prove it in a very efficient, if unbusinesslike manner.

* * * * *

Harlequin is 60 years old,
and Harlequin Blaze is celebrating!
After all, a lot can happen in 60 years,
or 60 minutes…or 60 seconds!
Find out what's going down in Blaze's
heart-stopping new miniseries,
FROM 0 TO 60!
Getting from "Hello" to "How was it?"
can happen fast….

Here's a sneak peek at the first book,
A LONG, HARD RIDE
by Alison Kent
Available March 2009

"Is that for me?" Trey asked.

Cardin Worth cocked her head to the side and considered how much better the day already seemed. "Good morning to you, too."

When she didn't hold out the second cup of coffee for him to take, he came closer. She sipped from her heavy white mug, hiding her grin and her giddy rush of nerves behind it.

But when he stopped in front of her, she made the mistake of lowering her gaze from his face to the exposed strip of his chest. It was either give him his cup of coffee or bury her nose against him and breathe in. She remembered so clearly how he smelled. How he tasted.

She gave him his coffee.

After taking a quick gulp, he smiled and said, "Good morning, Cardin. I hope the floor wasn't too hard for you."

The hardness of the floor hadn't been the problem. She shook her head. "Are you kidding? I slept like a baby, swaddled in my sleeping bag."

"In my sleeping bag, you mean."

If he wanted to get technical, yeah. "Thanks for the

loaner. It made sleeping on the floor almost bearable."
As had the warmth of his spooned body, she thought,
then quickly changed the subject. "I saw you have a loaf
of bread and some eggs. Would you like me to cook
breakfast?"

He lowered his coffee mug slowly, his gaze as warm
as the sun on her shoulders, as the ceramic heating her
hands. "I didn't bring you out here to wait on me."

"You didn't bring me out here at all. I volunteered to
come."

"To help me get ready for the race. Not to serve me."

"It's just breakfast, Trey. And coffee." Even if last
night it had been more. Even if the way he was looking
at her made her want to climb back into that sleeping
bag. "I work much better when my stomach's not
growling. I thought it might be the same for you."

"It is, but I'll cook. You made the coffee."

"That's because I can't work at all without caffeine."

"If I'd known that, I would've put on a pot as soon
as I got up."

"What time *did* you get up?" Judging by the sun's
position, she swore it couldn't be any later than seven
now. And, yeah, they'd agreed to start working at six.

"Maybe four?" he guessed, giving her a lazy smile.

"But it was almost two…" She let the sentence
dangle, finishing the thought privately. She was quite
sure he knew exactly what time they'd finally fallen
asleep after he'd made love to her.

The question facing her now was where did this relationship—if you could even call it *that*—go from here?

* * * * *

Cardin and Trey are about to find out that great sex is only the beginning....
Don't miss the fireworks!
Get ready for
A LONG, HARD RIDE
by Alison Kent
Available March 2009,
wherever Blaze books are sold.

CELEBRATE
60 YEARS
OF PURE READING PLEASURE
WITH HARLEQUIN®!

**We'll be spotlighting a different series
every month throughout 2009
to celebrate our 60th anniversary.**

Look for Harlequin® Blaze™ in March!

0-60

*After all, a lot can happen in 60 years,
or 60 minutes...or 60 seconds!*

Find out what's going down in Blaze's
heart-stopping new miniseries *0-60!*
Getting from "Hello" to "How was it?"
can happen fast....

Look for the brand-new 0-60 miniseries in March 2009!

HARLEQUIN® Romance®

This February the Harlequin® Romance series
will feature six Diamond Brides stories featuring
diamond proposals and gorgeous grooms.

Share your dream wedding
proposal and you could WIN!

The most romantic entry will win a diamond
necklace and will inspire a proposal in one of
our upcoming Diamond Grooms books in 2010.

In 100 words or less, tell us the most romantic
way that you dream of being proposed to.

For more information, and to enter
the Diamond Brides Proposal contest, please visit
www.DiamondBridesProposal.com

Or mail your entry to us at:
IN THE U.S.: 3010 Walden Ave., P.O. Box 9069, Buffalo, NY 14269-9069
IN CANADA: 225 Duncan Mill Road, Don Mills, ON M3B 3K9

REQUEST YOUR FREE BOOKS!

2 FREE NOVELS PLUS 2 FREE GIFTS!

Passionate, Powerful, Provocative!

YES! Please send me 2 FREE Silhouette Desire® novels and my 2 FREE gifts (gifts are worth about $10). After receiving them, if I don't wish to receive any more books, I can return the shipping statement marked "cancel". If I don't cancel, I will receive 6 brand-new novels every month and be billed just $4.05 per book in the U.S. or $4.74 per book in Canada, plus 25¢ shipping and handling per book and applicable taxes, if any*. That's a savings of almost 15% off the cover price! I understand that accepting the 2 free books and gifts places me under no obligation to buy anything. I can always return a shipment and cancel at any time. Even if I never buy another book, the two free books and gifts are mine to keep forever.

225 SDN ERVX 326 SDN ERVM

Name	(PLEASE PRINT)	
Address		Apt. #
City	State/Prov.	Zip/Postal Code

Signature (if under 18, a parent or guardian must sign)

Mail to the Silhouette Reader Service:
IN U.S.A.: P.O. Box 1867, Buffalo, NY 14240-1867
IN CANADA: P.O. Box 609, Fort Erie, Ontario L2A 5X3

Not valid to current subscribers of Silhouette Desire books.

Want to try two free books from another line?
Call 1-800-873-8635 or visit www.morefreebooks.com.

* Terms and prices subject to change without notice. N.Y. residents add applicable sales tax. Canadian residents will be charged applicable provincial taxes and GST. Offer not valid in Quebec. This offer is limited to one order per household. All orders subject to approval. Credit or debit balances in a customer's account(s) may be offset by any other outstanding balance owed by or to the customer. Please allow 4 to 6 weeks for delivery. Offer available while quantities last.

Your Privacy: Silhouette Books is committed to protecting your privacy. Our Privacy Policy is available online at www.eHarlequin.com or upon request from the Reader Service. From time to time we make our lists of customers available to reputable third parties who may have a product or service of interest to you. If you would prefer we not share your name and address, please check here. ☐

SDES08R

You're invited to join our Tell Harlequin Reader Panel!

By joining our new reader panel you will:

- Receive Harlequin® books—they are FREE and yours to keep with no obligation to purchase anything!
- Participate in fun online surveys
- Exchange opinions and ideas with women just like you
- Have a say in our new book ideas and help us publish the best in women's fiction

In addition, you will have a chance to win great prizes and receive special gifts!
See Web site for details. Some conditions apply.
Space is limited.

To join, visit us at
www.TellHarlequin.com.

COMING NEXT MONTH
Available March 10, 2009

#1927 THE MORETTI HEIR—Katherine Garbera
Man of the Month
The one woman who can break his family's curse proposes a contract: she'll have his baby, but love must *not* be part of the bargain.

#1928 TALL, DARK...WESTMORELAND!—Brenda Jackson
The Westmorelands
Surprised when he discovers his secret lover's true identity, this Westmoreland will stop at nothing to get her back into his bed!

#1929 TRANSFORMED INTO THE FRENCHMAN'S MISTRESS—Barbara Dunlop
The Hudsons of Beverly Hills
She needs a favor, and he's determined to use that to his advantage. He'll give her what she wants *if* she agrees to his request and stays under his roof.

#1930 SECRET BABY, PUBLIC AFFAIR—Yvonne Lindsay
Rogue Diamonds
Their affair was front-page news, yet her pregnancy was still top secret. When he's called home to Tuscany and demands she join him, will passion turn to love?

#1931 IN THE ARGENTINE'S BED—Jennifer Lewis
The Hardcastle Progeny
He'll give her his DNA in exchange for a night in his bed. But even the simplest plans can lead to the biggest surprises....

#1932 FRIDAY NIGHT MISTRESS—Jan Colley
Publicly they were fierce enemies, yet in private, their steamy affair was all that he craved. Could their relationship evolve into something beyond their Friday night trysts?

SDCNMBPA0209